DIGGING DEEP

An erotic novella

Kay Jaybee

Published by Xcite Books – 2013
ISBN 9781909840089

Copyright © Kay Jaybee 2013

The right of Kay Jaybee to be identified as the author of this work has been asserted by her in accordance with the Copyright, Designs and Patents Act 1988.

The story contained within this book is a work of fiction. Names and characters are the product of the author's imagination and any resemblance to actual persons, living or dead, is entirely coincidental.

All rights reserved. No part of this book may be copied, or transmitted in any form or by any means, electronic, electrostatic, magnetic tape, mechanical, photocopying, recording or otherwise, without the written permission of the publishers: Xcite Books, Suite 11769, 2nd Floor, 145-157 St John Street, London EC1V 4PY

Digging Deep is dedicated to all the archaeologists who have worked on the amazing Lepti Minus site over the years. What fun we had …

Chapter One

Irritably adjusting her wide-brimmed hat for the third time in as many minutes, Dr Beth Andrews felt the sting of the African sun sear the back of her neck through the tresses of her long, ginger hair.

She never dreamt she'd miss the stubborn, muddy clay of the British earth she was used to hunting through in her search for archaeological data, but the uncooperatively fine white sand of North Africa was enough to try the patience of a saint.

Throwing down her brush in overheated exasperation, Beth thought fondly of her excavation trowel. Her tool of choice had quickly been rendered obsolete in the face of so much sand, and a job that was, by necessity, slow was reduced to a snail's pace as the metre by metre square of the Ancient Roman bath house site in which she worked backfilled in on itself with every sweep of her light bristled brush.

It had been a dream come true for Beth when she'd been selected to lead the University of Wales's excavation team, digging the sprawling Ancient Roman city of Lepti Major on the outskirts of Sousse in Tunisia. She had longed to experience new exotic sites and see new exotic sights. The chance to uncover stunning mosaics and city roads that hadn't been trodden for 1000 years was an opportunity she'd had no intention of letting pass by.

The fact she'd be sharing responsibility for the site with her archaeological hero, the unimaginatively named Dr Harrison Harris from Colorado, an American academic who'd been the subject of many of Beth's private fantasies since she'd fallen in love with his work, not to mention the photograph of him on the back cover of his books, in her first year as a student, was neither here nor there.

Flicking her eyes covertly over towards Harrison, Beth averted her attention away from the slight increase in her pulse rate by recalling what the site's previous supervisor had said about working in Africa's extreme temperatures. "Scalding by day, and freezing by night". Linda had warned Beth that her freckle-spotted, sensitive flesh would loathe being either fried or frozen just as much as her archaeological brain would relish the challenge of constructing a city from its remains.

Beth hated the fact that Linda had been right. She'd never been rendered so sweaty, not to mention so blotched with extra heat-induced freckles, in her life. There couldn't have been a centimetre of her body that hadn't got a fresh cluster of beige dots on it. After only a week under the sun, it was becoming a struggle to hold on to her generally calm approach to life, and Beth was finding that her temper, which rarely flared in the UK, was on a permanently short fuse.

What got to her most was that none of her colleagues seemed to be suffering at all. They were all happily tanning as they worked, and sleeping off their exhaustion with ease at night.

It hadn't taken Beth more than a few hours of digging in the unshaded bath house on her first day to see that a survival technique was required to prevent the elements disrupting her professional judgement. She tried thinking about work, home, rain, and even walks in the snow as she worked, but only one thing successfully diverted her attention from the exposure of her unusually pale flesh to the elements, and that was to allow her mind to fill with erotic scenarios and fantasies, while her fingers got on with the job in hand.

This specialised amusement had the benefit of taking her mind off the sun that managed to scald her back even through three layers of thin cotton, and had the added bonus of warming her at night. Lying on her thin camping mattress, Beth would recall all she'd pondered during the day, engendering an ardour between her thighs that her fingers deftly maximised, leaving her physically warmer and bodily sated, and thus making it easier for her to fall asleep.

At first, Beth had been determined that Harrison would not feature in her erotic musings. Her resolve had not lasted long, however, and although she did her best to make the men in her sexy survival scenarios anonymous, the American's face crept in with increasing frequency.

Manoeuvring a layer of burning sand from one side of her section to the other, Beth considered her colleague. His reputation as an expert in Roman archaeology was renowned. Beth had never dreamt she'd ever meet him, let alone work with him as an equal. His knowledge and academic intellect had been enough to make her heart flutter for years. Yet what Harrison was like in reality was not at all how she'd assumed he'd be.

She'd envisaged him as being chatty, tall, slim, dark-haired, and weather-tanned. He'd probably wear glasses for reading, and be forever clad in T-shirts and large-pocketed shorts as he leapt around excavations like a gazelle.

In fact, she'd hardly heard Harrison's distinct Colorado accent. He seemed to prefer his own company to that of the group. When he did talk to Beth, he called her "doll," which made her feel like a lump of mass-produced, animated plastic.

Harrison was about 5 foot 7, not the 6 foot plus she'd pictured, and his spiked hair was a sun-kissed blond and not brown. His build was stocky and muscular, his bare arms and legs permanently gritted with granules of sand, and although he moved with a speed which would have been the envy of any gazelle, he managed to proceed around the site somehow without making a sound.

The problem is, Beth thought as she traced the outline of what she suspected might be a Roman drain gully, I built up an image of him based on a book cover's black-and-white out of date headshot, and I was way off.

She'd been right about Harrison wearing knee-length shorts, though. Everyone on the dig wore such shorts, except for the stick thin, heavy-chested blonde on the American team, who might as well have been wearing knickers her shorts were so scanty. Beth sighed as she looked down at her own attire. A protective covering of baggy clothing shrouded her limbs, and her porcelain neck was hidden beneath spirals of her ginger hair, which glowed as if she'd been hit by radiation rather than African sunlight.

Ryan wasn't helping either. The most charismatic of her students had been so enthusiastic on his first morning that he'd headed to the site before everybody else, without waiting for Beth to detail where to dig. Consequently, he'd powered through the ground in an alarmingly gung-ho manner, neglected the recording of each strata-graphic layer and, with his six-pack and biceps shining against 120 degrees of sunshine, had crashed his shovel into the corner of a mosaic that had been safely protected by the landscape for hundreds of years, breaking off half-a-dozen exquisitely coloured tessera tiles, and rendering one of the depicted Medusa's snakes partially headless.

Beth had gone ballistic. To his credit, Ryan had been mortified. He'd begged her not to tell anyone. For the sake of the university's reputation, not to mention her fear that Harrison would take one look at her careless student, assume she was no good at supervision, and send her home, she had agreed it would be their secret. Ever since, however, Ryan had been driving Beth mad with his attempts to make it up to her at every opportunity.

Only that morning he'd lent so close to Beth as he informed her he was going to make up for his blunder that his soft Welsh tones had vibrated against her skin. His manner was so blatantly suggestive that she hadn't been able to prevent the inappropriate smile that had very briefly crossed her lips.

Picking up her dustpan and brush, Beth stroked away the grains of sand that sat between her and her judgement as to whether the lines being revealed were part of the bath house drainage system or not. Expertly tracing the changing colours in the freshly uncovered ground, Beth, confident that her theory was correct, and that the ancient shadows of the gully she could see could be followed across the ground with ease, readopted her technique to deviate her attention from the cruel climate, while her fingers worked the earth.

What exactly is Ryan offering? she wondered. A sneaky snog behind the equipment cupboard? A cooling down of my chest with his tongue? Or is he more ambitious than that? Does he imagine me naked, face down, spread-eagled over an empty wheelbarrow with his cock between my legs; or see us together in the shower, washing off the worst of the sand that seems to be permanently stuck to my body while he shoves his dick down my throat?

For goodness' sake, woman! she chided herself. Beth was surprised to find her chest, whose generous size she'd always loved before, but now heartily wished was small enough to go without the extra layer of material her bra provided, was becoming taut. Cross with herself, she shook her hair out from beneath her hat, as if trying to dislodge the thoughts from her head. Having random erotic dreams might be the only thing that keeps you sane in this blast furnace – but you must *not* consider your students! Get a grip!

Briskly returning to the matter in hand, Beth cut through a layer of denser sand, wishing Ryan wasn't working the section directly behind her. She daren't turn to check he was all right like she did her other students. The last time she'd done so, she had caught him ogling her butt with a suggestive wiggle of his eyebrows, which couldn't have been mistaken for anything other than the type of lustful intentions her own imagination had just so colourfully displayed to her. Ever since then, she had been more than a little self-conscious of the stretch of her cotton combats over her backside.

Crouching on her haunches, letting her eyes roam across the site as a whole, Beth struck Ryan from her mind, and began weighing up the significance of what she was excavating in relation to what else was opening up on the dig before her. As she leant in closer, a glitter of something just below the upper level of the sand caught her eye. Trailing her brush across the yellow surface, she mentally listed all the hidden things that might shine: mosaic tesserae, jewellery, votive offerings to the gods ...

With a sharp scream, Beth stumbled backwards out of her square in a mad scramble to escape. Her find was none of the things archaeologists dream of uncovering. In the haste to get away, her left foot caught on the guide string that divided her metre section from the next. Tripping, she fell heavily backwards.

Flushed with an embarrassment that enflamed her already pinkened features, Beth found herself being scooped onto Ryan's lap, his arms wrapped protectively around her.

Alerted by the unexpected shriek, the other students in the immediate vicinity began to gather round. Most of them, however, backed away the moment they saw what had caused Beth's unusual lack of professionalism; except for the leggy American, who looked at Ryan in disgust, pointedly rolled her eyes at Beth, and returned to her work.

Beth didn't have time to think about the blonde's unsympathetic reaction. All her attention was on the bronze snake which hadn't appreciated its home being disturbed by an inquisitive human. She was convinced it was staring straight at her, its tongue flicking, smelling the air around it in an accusatory manner.

Her initial shock subsiding, and abruptly sensible of where she was, and how it must appear to see one of the supervisors in the embrace of a student, Beth scrambled shakily to her feet. She wasn't sure if she was more mortified by her public reaction to the snake, or by the fact that her body felt more than a little content at being cradled so protectively in Ryan's arms so recently after her erotic ruminations had headed in his direction. 'I'm sorry, everyone! That was a bit of a shock. I'm not good with snakes.'

'Don't worry about it, boss.' Ryan ran a consoling hand down Beth's cotton-covered arm, creating small prickles of uninvited lust that appeared on top of the prickles of fear already there, and sending them both tripping towards her crotch.

Rueing her kinky imagination, Beth took another step away from her student. Moving rather too fast, she collided with the stocky frame of Harrison Harris. He'd crossed the site on his ever-silent feet to see what all the fuss was about without her even noticing, causing Beth to jump out of her skin for a second time. 'Honestly, Harrison, don't you ever make a sound when you move?'

'Hardly ever!' He treated her to one of his Colorado smiles, making Beth suspect that he was privately laughing at her. 'You OK, doll?'

Not stopping to waste her breath on asking him for the umpteenth time not to call her "doll", Beth did her best to ignore the twinkle in Harrison's eye that confirmed he found the situation hilarious, and settled for being grateful that he hadn't vocalised his mirth in front of their charges.

'I'm fine. The snake took me by surprise.'

Beth had no doubt this little episode would be site folklore by dinner time. She didn't usually care about that sort of thing, and was always one of the first to laugh when she made a fool of herself, but now she found her face darkening with embarrassment in the face of her colleague.

'Is that all?' Harrison bent down and retrieved the brush Beth had abandoned in her hurry to move away from the snake. 'You're sure?'

'I'm sure. Just shock. I don't like snakes. I haven't damaged anything, I hope.'

'No harm done.' Harrison shot Ryan a look which

plainly said "this time", making Beth wonder if the timing of the breaking of the mosaic had gone unnoticed after all. 'Here you go, doll.' He gestured to the creature. 'He's just a sand snake. Won't do you any harm. I'll move him somewhere safe.'

'Thank you.' Beth's words came out rather weakly as the unfortunate creature was picked up and repositioned against a dune of previously excavated sand, into which it quickly disappeared. Seeing Harrison rehome the creature with no more fuss than if he'd moved a worm from a flower bed to a vegetable patch made Beth even more cross with herself for being so feeble in front of a man she'd so badly wanted to impress. She found herself babbling in explanation, 'Insects I have no problem with. Spiders are cool. But snakes ... I can't stand them.'

This time Harrison did laugh openly, wiping one of his calloused palms across his forehead, smearing dirt into his spiky hair and knocking back his faded Stetson in the process. 'You're a regular Indiana Jones, doll!'

Keen to keep the general atmosphere light, Beth added, 'Well. As long as I don't get chased by any oversized boulders or attacked by a tribe of pygmies with blowpipes then I guess I can live with the comparison!'

Taking a hefty swig from her water bottle, she smiled, relieved that her ability to laugh at herself was finally reasserting itself after days of being diminished by the heat.

Harrison grinned as he strolled to his side of the dig. 'Gotta love that dry English sense of humour, doll.'

Beth called after him, 'Thanks for the snake removal, Harry.'

He kept walking as he corrected her. 'Harrison. It's Harrison, I told you. I don't like being called Harry.'

She shouted at his retreating back, 'And I don't like being referred to as a doll. It makes me sound like a character in an American B-movie! Message received?'

Still laughing, Harrison didn't look round, but held up a hand as if in defeat. 'Gotcha, doll! Message received.'

Stepping back into her square, Beth looked at her watch. It wasn't even ten o'clock in the morning, and the heat was already making it feel as if someone was systematically pouring paint stripper across her shoulders. She could hear her students chatting happily as they worked. All except for Ryan, who was unusually quiet.

Beth sighed as she recalled Harrison's glare towards Ryan, and realised it wasn't just her rationale she'd left in the colder climate of home, but her common sense as well. It was time to come clean about how Ryan had messed up the mosaic and, more importantly, why she hadn't reported the incident straight away.

Her decision made, Beth's hands returned to working the ground, while her imagination speculated how it might have felt if Harrison had been the one she'd accidentally sat on. *Would I have wanted to get up quite so quickly?* Her pussy twitched as if in confirmation, as her green eyes studied the Roman drain …

Chapter Two

Hidden away in the garden at the rear of the house they were staying in, taking advantage of a few moments' peace between the end of the morning's digging and lunch, Harrison rested his back against the shaded trunk of a large-leafed palm tree. He'd told himself he was there so he could update his notes without being disturbed, but he knew he was really just avoiding Beth.

He screwed his eyes up against the ideas that seemed to circle on continuous loop through his head. She is a decade younger than me, lives in another continent, and is a colleague. So don't even think about it! Determined not to contradict this train of thought with reminders of how badly he wanted to find out how far Beth's freckles travelled across her body, what the spring of her russet ringlets would feel like in his fingers, or speculate about how she seemed to make him laugh even when the most ordinary words came out of her mouth in her cute English accent, Harrison had decided to keep as much distance between himself and Beth as possible. It would help if she wasn't so damn good at her job.

He sighed hard. Work relationships were never a good idea – especially when they were only destined to work together for three months of the year! His year with Linda, Beth's predecessor, had proved that. Anyway, such indiscretions were unprofessional, and Harrison had always prided himself on his professionalism.

As he urged himself to stop contemplating why Beth, in her multiple layers of clothing, felt more attractive to him than any of the semi-clad females who worked around the site, Harrison suddenly sensed that he wasn't alone. Lifting his head from his notes, he saw Candida lounging against the wall on the opposite side of the dust-soiled garden.

His heart sank. Of all his students, she was the last person he felt like talking to. For a second, Harrison assumed she'd been looking for him, but swallowed a muted murmur of relief when she faced the other way, and tapped urgently against the touch screen of her phone.

Intent on staying focused on the report he was writing, Harrison sat silently against the side of the house, hoping that his student wouldn't spot him. Bending his head to his work, Harrison snapped it up again as Candida's grating voice echoed around the small, square garden.

'Of course I'm not ignoring your calls.'

Raising his eyebrows, he immediately felt sorry for whoever was at the other end of the phone. Candida might well have been a sight for sore eyes with her rounded chest, flat stomach, and tanned legs that seemed to go on for ever, but her voice was enough to scour the varnish off wood, and her "I'm beautiful and therefore you will love me" attitude was proof, if any was needed, that Candida Harker was Daddy's little princess through and through. Not for the first time, Harrison cursed that the "daddy" in question was the owner of Harker International, the company providing most of the sponsorship for the dig, and so her presence on the team was secured each time Colorado University came to the site.

Harrison's attempts to ignore the rest of her conversation were abruptly halted as Candida pronounced down the phone, 'Well, you were right. She should have an eye kept on her. Who'd have thought it of someone so mousy and dull? I mean, she is so white and spotty she could be mistaken for the ghost of a leopard!'

There was a break from Candida's high-decibel yakking, as whoever was on the other end of the call spoke, before she responded, 'Well, yes, it seems she does have some sort of MILF quality. I tell you, *no* American guy would humiliate himself like that with anyone who wasn't at least of goddess status. Which she most certainly is not! And not because he was in her debt!'

Trying not to care which of the English students Candida was ripping apart, and hoping like hell that everyone else was out of earshot of her diatribe, Harrison frowned as his student went on.

'Supervisory skills? How the hell should I know? I'm on Harrison's team, thank God. And will not be swapping under any circumstances.'

Harrison's head jerked back up, his ears straining for information. *Beth?* She was bad-mouthing Beth. *Why?* He didn't dare even rustle his papers, although he was sure Candida was so involved in her call that an entire herd of elephants could go by and she wouldn't notice.

'Yes, I know, but I don't want …'

There was an odd hint of panic in his student's voice now, and Harrison began to wish that the person on the other end of the phone was as loud as Candida, so he could hear whatever it was they were saying.

'OK – well, I wasn't going to tell you this …'

Like hell. Harrison recognised when Candida was building up to spill some slanderous scandal.

'I don't think it is her ability as an archaeologist that is in question. It is her relationship with her students. With one student in particular.'

A vision of Beth's flushed face as she sat on Ryan's lap, after the snake had frightened her, flashed through Harrison's brain.

Candida was nodding in satisfaction, her previously concerned countenance replaced with one of smug relief. 'Yes. Yes, that's right.'

Harrison closed his eyes. Who the hell was on the end of that line? He gripped his papers, physically having to stop himself from getting up and ripping the cell phone from Candida's hand so he could challenge the unseen recipient.

'Well, OK, but it isn't pretty.' Candida paused as if for dramatic effect, as Harrison impatiently waited to hear what her *coup de grâce* against his colleague was going to be. A feeling of foreboding crept ever faster up his spine as he heard her say, 'One of her students is fucking her in return for her silence.'

Harrison felt as though he'd swallowed an orange whole as a triumphant Candida went on. 'Yes! Every day! Just so she won't tell anyone he broke the mosaic he was excavating. Apparently, yesterday lunchtime Beth made Ryan beg! Can you credit it! She actually made him *beg*! And all that time the bitch was naked and getting a good time up on the open roof. Fuck! I mean, what would she have made him do if he'd smashed the whole thing, and not just crumbled the edge a bit?'

With the use of Beth's name, the last vestige of hope that Harrison had been mistaken about what he'd heard evaporated. It isn't true, he told himself. It can't be – can it? But what is Candida up to? His appetite for lunch disappeared as, with morbid fascination, he continued to listen ...

Four hours later, observing the half-exposed tiles through the sand before him, Harrison told himself, for the umpteenth time, that what Candida had said down her cell phone was total rubbish. He'd misunderstood, having only heard one side of the conversation. Although there was no way he could have misread the relieved smugness on Candida's face when she'd gone on to detail the depths of Beth's supposed depravity, and Ryan's own motives.

Despite every vestige of his common sense telling him it was ludicrous, the conversation he'd accidentally eavesdropped wouldn't stop bugging him. Candida's words whirred around Harrison's head. The thought of Beth having a sexual relationship with Ryan amplified the recurring vision of her sat, albeit by accident, in the lap of her most musclebound student, driving him to distraction.

It had to be rubbish. But the mosaic had been broken ... Why was Candida dishing the dirt on two people she hardly knew?

Consulting his watch, Harrison was surprised to see it was almost time to close the site for the day. Aside from his personal preoccupations, archaeologically it had been a fairly productive day. The outline of the increasingly opulent bath house was beginning to take on a very impressive shape.

This was his third season on the site, and although the Tunisian authorities only allowed it to be opened for four months of the year, Harrison felt he'd come to know the excavation well. Last season, he and Linda had uncovered a skeleton-packed mausoleum, and the year before that they'd worked on the city's forum.

Harrison was looking forward to adding the outline

of the bathing area to the city plans, and had already begun planning the chapters he'd write about the bath house when the book about the excavation was written. He'd intended to ask Beth to help him compile the book now that Linda had been promoted and was, thank God, out of his life. Now he wasn't so sure.

Harrison knew his fair share of ambitious people, but Linda won the prize. He couldn't believe he'd been such a blind fool where she was concerned. That wasn't a mistake he was *ever* going to make again.

Tapping the end of his brush against his palm, he surveyed the Roman hypocaust heating system that had once warmed the bath waters; his mind, however, was on something quite different from this amazing innovation.

Memories of Linda, all business, nifty trowel action, and deceivingly girly pigtails, which hid an underlying dangerous ambition, elbowed their way into Harrison's consciousness alongside the stains of Candida's gossip. The woman was fast heading towards being the youngest female Professor of Archaeology in the UK, by whatever means possible. And he had been one of those "means".

Harrison poked pointlessly at the ground as he recalled their two African seasons together. It had seemed so romantic, working under the sun all day and cuddling up together at night. He'd liked Linda. A lot. He'd let her get under his skin, and would have done anything for her, right up until the point when the penny had dropped and he'd realised he was merely a stepping stone on her road to academic achievement.

As his head filled up with images of their dig-time fling, which had been physically highly rewarding but had ended up costing him his own hopes of climbing the career ladder, Harrison squashed down the anger her felt at his own naivety. He'd been delighted when Beth had replaced Linda. He'd believed the nightmare would be over. It appeared he was wrong. He'd put money on Linda being on the other end of that call with Candida, but for the life of him, he couldn't think why.

Taking a gathering breath, Harrison forced himself to consider more immediate worries. He'd assumed it had been a local who'd broken the mosaic in a pointless hunt for saleable treasure. Surely Beth would have said if she had known it was Ryan who'd damaged it?

Beth was young, and Harrison knew this was her first foreign dig as supervisor, albeit in a post holding joint responsibility with his own. She was an experienced archaeologist who'd come highly recommended by her university department. He just couldn't square the Beth he was working alongside with someone who'd be so unprofessional as to cover up a blunder like that. Unless, of course, she was having an affair with him …

Straightening up, Harrison gave the order for his students to down tools. *No. It isn't true. It can't be.* Fed up with pointlessly going around in circles, Harrison decided to trust his own instincts rather than Candida. He credited Beth with far more taste, and a great deal more common sense. No way would she sleep with one of her students. No way.

He glanced across the site towards Beth, and instantly Harrison's brain reverted to the very thoughts he'd just dismissed. The image of his associate entwined in Ryan's arms became increasingly lurid, and he couldn't stop himself from visualising the scenarios that Candida had so gleefully expounded to her contact.

Her ginger curls jumping against her back, Harrison could vividly see Beth standing proud with Ryan on his knees before her. Her naked body was a startling white, in contrast to her student's bronzed flesh. Her ample tits were swollen under Ryan's grasp ... He squeezed his eyes shut, trying to banish the tableau that Candida had planted in his head, yet he was helpless to stop visions of a nude Ryan, his dick rock hard, pleading with his boss to be allowed to plunge into her body.

Candida's begrudging respect echoed in Harrison's head again and again. "Apparently, yesterday lunchtime Beth made Ryan beg! Can you credit it! She actually made the guy beg! And all that time the bitch was naked and getting a good time up on the open roof ..."

Annoyed at himself for even half-believing Candida, Harrison couldn't shift his feelings of suspicion. After all, Beth might be a complete cutie, with her polite way of talking, and her bouncy curls, who knew her way around a dig blindfold, but that didn't mean she was a good person. He realised that he didn't know Beth at all. She could just be another Linda ... It could all be true. She and Ryan did pot-wash alone on the house roof yesterday. They could have got up to anything ...

Trying to concentrate on closing the site for the night, telling himself sternly that all this would be cleared up later that evening, and he'd undoubtedly discover that Candida was spinning a web of lies, Harrison strode over to a pile of buckets and brushes to dump his tools.

Again he looked beyond his own workers towards the British team. The light, even though it was late in the day, still semi-blinded him as he made out the slim curviness of his co-supervisor.

A grin crossed his face.

Of course! There was no way it could be true. Harrison nodded to himself as he regarded Beth, clad from top to toe in layers of light cotton, recognising that he'd felt disappointed in her without any grounds to feel that way beyond gossip. Beth would never expose her skin to the elements in the way Candida described.

From the moment Dr Andrews had stepped off the plane at Tunis airport, apart from her face and a tiny patch of skin on her neck, which Harrison noticed seemed to constantly escape the shielding of her hat's brim, she had been covered from head to toe in long, baggy trousers, and full sleeved T-shirts to protect her porcelain skin.

Harrison smiled as he considered how, even though they'd worked together for a week now, it was still a shock each evening when Beth removed the top swathe of fabric and her hat, revealing her uncontrollable curls and alabaster arms, which were so spotted with freckles that a join the dots freak would have been kept happy for years.

There was absolutely no way Beth would be so careful about protecting herself, and then recklessly expose her burnable chest during the hottest part of the day, even if Ryan had had the pleasure of lathering it in a whole bottle worth of factor 50 sun cream.

The second Harrison thought about Beth's chest and the application of cream, he wished he hadn't. He couldn't stop picturing what her breasts might be like, or how it might feel to apply lotion to them.

As he began to head back to the house, Harrison pulled himself together. This is just good old fashioned lust, he conceded. She has a nice chest, and I am fantasising about it. Nothing odd in that. It has nothing at all to do with me fancying Beth. Absolutely nothing! Because I don't.

Already in the process of closing her side of the excavation for the night, Beth wiped her hands down her trousers. For once, the sunshine and work-induced sweat was not responsible for the slick coating of perspiration on her palms.

For hours she'd been mulling over how on earth she was going to tell Harrison about the fact she knew Ryan had broken the mosaic, but hadn't said anything. She felt anxious just thinking about it, especially given the strange glances her co-supervisor had been giving her on and off all afternoon. Beth hoped the quizzical, downright disapproving stares were just because she was frightened of snakes and he thought her a wimp; but she suspected there was more to them than that.

With the sinking feeling that one of the archaeologists she most respected was about to be very disappointed in her, Beth followed her happily chatting students at a discreet distance back to the partly built house in which they were lodging, watching as Ryan ran to catch up Candida, and quickly engaged her in conversation.

Beth tried not to hear the words of the students nearest to her as they walked, but the clear air made sound travel all too easily, and she picked up the words "snakes" and "clumsy" whether she wanted to hear them or not. She didn't need to see Ryan to know he'd have a smooth expression on his face, although the reason behind the glance of pure poison that Candida gave her, as she and Ryan muttered to one another, was totally lost on Beth.

Easing the cotton layers from her neck a fraction, in a pointless attempt to circulate air against her flesh, Beth decided she needed some time out. As soon as they were in the relative cool of the house, she would escape from everyone for a while, take her meal to her room, and plan how on earth she was going to tell Harrison about the mosaic while persuading him not to send her, and her students, home.

Chapter Three

'Fancy strolling down to the olive fields, doll? I'd like to pace out the area so we can get some field-walking teams set up. We could fill each other in on the day as we go.'

Too wound up by how her confession would be received when she made it, Beth didn't bother to admonish Harrison for calling her "doll" again. Pulling on a second jumper as protection against the growing chill of the evening, she gathered up the few notes she'd made. 'Good idea. The sooner we get that task started the better.'

In her room, Beth had imagined herself and Harrison sitting at the table in the dining room while she apologised for not telling him about Ryan's clumsiness, pleading with him not to report her to her head of department back in Wales. Perhaps this way is better, she thought, to be away from the prying eyes and ears of any of the students who still had the energy to be up.

For the eighth night on the trot, Beth marvelled at how the temperature could go from one level of unbearable and head towards another in such a short space of time. She knew they only had about two hours before the jumper she wore wouldn't be enough to hold out the night-time cold.

Walking in silence, the lack of conversation hanging heavily between them, Beth frantically considered what to say, the crunch of her walking boots against the stony pathway the only sound as she tried to match Harrison's giant, silent strides. In the end, she opted for a feeble, 'You have a good day, then?'

'Excellent, thanks.' Harrison regarded her with what could either be open interest or suspicion, and Beth felt her stomach contract beneath the hold of his clear blue eyes. 'We found the start of the hypocaust. Got some wonderfully intact box flue tiles.'

'That's wonderful!' Beth sighed. 'I'm sorry, Harrison, I meant to come over and examine your side of the site today, but I've been a bit preoccupied. My square is a bit complex. I suspect I have the drainage system kicking off, but I'm not sure yet which way it's going to flow for sure. I'd love to see your section on the way back if it's not too dark. Or maybe in the morning?'

Not allowing him time to chip in, scared of what he might go on to say, Beth went on with her monologue. 'If my theory is correct, the drainage system should run from my square, through the next two, and on into the unopened middle section towards you guys. I was going to suggest we clear the top level off the connecting earth by the end of the week? With your hypocaust evidence, it seems even more urgent to do that.'

Relieved to be talking shop, and even more relieved that Harrison was nodding in agreement with her, Beth ignored the voice at the back of her head telling her she had the man of her dreams all to herself and she was discussing drainage systems! Instead, she listened as Harrison detailed his own theory as to where the heating system and drains might run, and how the layout of the bath house was shaping up in general. Beth's relief came to an abrupt halt when Harrison added, with a less than casual air, that he was almost certain the broken

Medusa mosaic had once formed the floor of the cold room's plunge pool.

Glancing sideways at Beth, Harrison tried to gauge her reaction at the mention of the mosaic afresh. He wanted to give his colleague a chance to come clean without him trying to catch her out. When she remained silent, he prompted her further. 'It's such a shame it was damaged. Fresh damage too. I guess it was one of the locals hunting treasure, or maybe just a regular accident. Someone could easily trip over it, considering its position.'

As they arrived at the edge of the first olive field, Harrison glanced at Beth again, unsure if she'd make use of the opening he'd given her.

She sat down on a bank of dusty earth that surrounded the field, and gestured for Harrison to join her. 'I have a confession.'

Resisting the temptation to tell her he already knew about Ryan's deliberate act of vandalism, Harrison forced himself to wait and listen to all the details in her own words.

'I should have told you as soon as it had happened, but I was so embarrassed. I badly wanted you to think well of me and my students. I couldn't believe it when that happened on my very first day. I truly was going to tell you, but then ... Although, none of that's an excuse. I am a total fool ...'

'Doll! Slow down, you're babbling. Tell me what actually happened.' Harrison put down his pad of notes and shuffled round so he was facing Beth properly. 'Are you telling me you're the one who broke the mosaic?'

'God no! I know I can be clumsy sometimes, but not on site! The guys at home are always telling me off for being too careful.'

'Except when you're being attacked by snakes?' He

couldn't resist the gentle jibe, and gave Beth a half-smile of encouragement now that she was coming clean.

'Being surprised by snakes is not something that happens too much in Britain!' Beth realised she'd replied rather more curtly than she'd intended to as she saw Harrison battle to keep his countenance solemn. The glimmer in his eye betrayed his amusement at her dislike of slithery things. 'I'm sorry about the mosaic. I should have told you, but he begged me not to.'

'Ryan?'

'Yes.' Beth's forehead creased, and she studied Harrison. He was frustratingly unreadable. 'You knew? I guessed you'd worked it out.'

'I overheard one of my students telling a friend about it on her phone.'

'What?' Beth couldn't believe what she was hearing. 'You mean I've risked my job by not telling you, have protected him at what should be the start of a very promising career if he stops pratting about, and he's been shouting his mouth off to the other students anyway? That boy is the giddy limit!'

'He's the what?' Harrison laughed despite himself.

'It means he's a pain in the arse!'

'You mean a pain the *ass*.' Harrison flashed his eyes at her again as he corrected her English into American, tempted to tell her that she looked beautiful when she was angry, but resisting, as he was sure it would earn him a slap.

Beth felt flustered as well as cross. She'd geared herself up to more or less beg for Harrison's forgiveness, for him to give her the chance to prove herself as a competent supervisor, and now they were sitting side by side in the twilight of an olive grove, and she was having to fight the urge to giggle. It would have been romantic if the situation wasn't so damn preposterous.

Struggling to keep to the confession she'd been building up to all day, Beth groaned, 'Oh for heaven's sake, an *ass* is a donkey, an *arse* is your butt!'

'Are you saying my nether regions resemble a donkey in some way?'

Beth went pink as she failed in her determination not to think about whether Harrison was hung like a donkey or not, and turned away from the flash of devilment that shone in his face. 'Honestly! I'm trying to clear my conscience here! I've been feeling guilty as hell for not telling you about Ryan.'

Harrison's jovial look died, and he visibly stiffened. 'Tell me what, *exactly,* about Ryan?'

Not caring for the stress he'd put on the word "exactly", Beth's nerves raced to her chest at top speed. 'That he broke the mosaic when he was showing off, of course. What else has he done?' Fiddling with a fallen olive, Beth powered on, 'It really was an accident. If I'd told you … I should have told you, but …'

'But you were afraid I'd think less of you, and you didn't want to damage Muscle Boy's career before it had even started.'

'Muscle Boy?' Beth felt her lips curling into a smile, causing some of the conflicting tensions within her to dissipate. 'Is that what you call him?'

'Only in my head.'

Beth repeated herself. 'He was showing off. When Ryan realised what he'd done he was beside himself. He begged me not to tell you. To be honest, I was so nervous about working with you, when that happened on day one I was convinced that if you knew you'd write me off as a useless waste of space and send me packing.'

'You're nuts, doll! Your reputation as an

archaeologist is excellent, and anyway, accidents happen.' Harrison shifted so he was studying her directly again, his gaze imploring. 'Is that all? There's nothing else going on with Ryan that I should know about?'

Beth ruffled her fingers through her already tangled hair. 'Not apart from the fact I'm getting sick to death of his attempts to make up for his blunder by being *way* too helpful and attentive.' She recalled how Ryan had refilled her water bottle constantly, been on hand to empty her buckets and barrows of sand, and generally made himself indispensable to the point of annoyance. 'Chivalry is all very well, but he's beginning to get annoying.'

The piercing nature of Harrison's steel blue eyes was beginning to unsettle her, and the tension she'd felt yo-yo around her system all day zipped through Beth's shoulder muscles as another disturbing thought occurred to her. 'Who did you overhear talking about the mosaic on the phone? Did they say how much of a gullible fool I was?'

Images of all the students sniggering at her expense suddenly filled Beth's head. Maybe they haven't been laughing at the snake episode, she thought. Maybe they have just been laughing at me in general? The limited colour in her complexion drained away, and she buried her head in her hands. 'I am gonna kill him!'

Now Harrison was worried. 'Doll? Are you OK, you said "gonna"?'

'Oh ha ha! That's it, why don't you join in and take the piss at my expense!'

'Doll?' Alarmed by Beth's blanched face and the sudden evaporation of her usual sense of self-deprecation, Harrison knew he'd been a fool to even entertain the thought that Candida had been telling the truth. No way had Beth done anything with Ryan except be stupidly kind. Reaching out a large hand, he placed it protectively on her knee, 'Beth?'

'No, I'm not flippin' all right! I don't appreciate being made to look foolish!' Pushing his hand away, Beth refused to let herself register that she immediately missed its comforting presence. She stood up and began to stride purposefully back to the house.

'Where you going, doll?'

'Where the hell do you think?' Anger lent wings to her feet as Beth marched onwards.

In silent pursuit, Harrison reached out and grabbed her shoulder, spinning Beth round so fast her boot soles squeaked against the earth. 'Will you cool it, doll; you don't have all the facts.'

'What the hell else is there to know? Ryan has made me appear a total pushover. And they –' Beth pointed vaguely in the direction of the house '– are all laughing at me. Great start to my first major dig as supervisor, I must say!'

'I told you! It wasn't Ryan I heard about the mosaic from, and I don't think anyone other than she and Ryan know.'

Standing stock still, Beth frowned. 'She? Which she?'

Steering Beth gently by the shoulder, Harrison guided her back to the olive field. 'Sit down; we have got to pace this lot out, remember.'

Taking a protracted exhalation of air, Beth found herself resting against the warmth of her colleague's side. 'Sorry. I overreacted. Tell me everything.'

Harrison spoke in a low hush. 'It was Candida. I heard her talking to someone on her phone.'

'Candida? She's the blonde one with legs up to her armpits?'

'That's the one. She also has, as you can't have failed to have noticed, a voice like a foghorn and a love of gossip, so it could be that some of the other students overheard her conversation as well.'

'Tell me the worst.'

Deciding she didn't need to hear everything he'd overheard, Harrison told her about Ryan's claims about breaking the mosaic as a backhanded way to sleep with her; taking the precaution of making sure he kept one hand fixed on Beth's arm to prevent her leaping up again and storming away in a fit of justifiable, but useless, temper.

As she listened, Beth began to shiver, but the chill that infused her was nothing to do with the cold of the approaching night. She spoke with an almost deadly calm. 'You believed her, didn't you? You believed what you heard. You decided that if I was capable of not telling you about Ryan's on-site stupidity, I was equally capable of blackmailing him for my silence with, with ...' She could hardly bring herself to say the words. 'With sex!'

Guilt flooded Harrison as he saw disappointment cloud Beth's eyes. 'Well, I couldn't help but wonder. I mean, Ryan has been all over you like a rash, and then, when I saw you sitting on his lap when that snake scared you ... I don't really know you, after all.'

'For fuck's sake! I fell! I sat on Ryan for only a few seconds.' Beth hadn't appreciated what it was like to seethe before – now she knew.

Harrison looked genuinely shocked, 'You swore! That's the first time I've heard you do that.'

'Of course I bloody swore! Wouldn't you? I'm not Mary bloody Poppins!'

Harrison held out his hands as if pleading for peace. 'Look, I'm sorry, OK!'

He got no further with his sentence. Beth pulled away from the clutch of his hand, and rose to her feet, her hands on her hips, her whole body shaking.

'You believed the word of a girl you tell me is famous for gossip, whose own parents have so little regard for her that they named her after a nasty fungal infection! How could you? How could you even think that I would ... With a student ...' Beth couldn't bring herself to repeat the words describing the scenarios Candida had invented. Forcing back the hypocritical guilt she felt about having a sexual fantasy about the young man in question earlier that day, she raged, 'I know I was wrong not to tell you about the mosaic. But not that. Never that!'

Harrison opened his mouth, but nothing he could think of to say seemed more than pathetic, placating words. Distress blazed in Beth's eyes. Suddenly, he understood just how big a deal this all was for her. Linda had told him that, apart from on site, where her ideas and theories were rarely wrong, Beth was quiet and lacked confidence in herself. The fact she'd been given the job as supervisor showed in what high esteem her head of department held her. Beth was, to quote Linda, "one to watch". There was no way she would risk messing up.

Harrison knew he should apologise, but here and now it seemed more important to stop her marching off at high speed and killing Ryan.

Beth was tugging against his hand, trying to escape and get back to the house. Without thinking about the consequences, Harrison held her tighter, and growled through gritted teeth, 'Oh for fuck's sake, Beth, I've said I'm sorry.'

Diving forward, he took her rage-red face in his free hand, and pulled her closer, kissing her fiercely on her bone-dry lips.

The first sensation Beth registered was that Harrison's stubble felt good as it scraped across her skin. The second was that she was being kissed by the man she'd idolised for years. For a moment, she relaxed into the kiss, enjoying its intensity, which was filling her up from the inside. Then reality hit her in a cold rush. Harrison didn't fancy her at all. He was just seeing if Candida was right; testing the theory that she would make out with anyone if it suited her situation. Humiliation took over from pleasure like a sharp kick in the teeth.

Yanking herself away, she glowered at her companion. 'What are trying to do? Prove I'm the slapper you think I am? Well, I am sorry to disappoint you, Dr Harris, but I am not that fucking easy. And yes, I did just bloody swear again, so please don't feel obliged to point it out.'

She couldn't stay where she was a moment longer. Forgetting about having to pace the olive groves, Beth pointed a finger directly at Harrison. 'Don't you dare follow me.' Then she walked back to the house with all the dignity she could muster, trying not to consider how incredible Harrison's kiss had felt against her lips.

Chapter Four

The scantily furnished three-storey house where the excavation team was lodging lay on the outskirts of Lepti Minus village, which sat side by side with its larger ancient sister settlement. The property's lack of doors, and windows without glass or shutters, kept it forever cool, and a blessed sanctuary from the blast of the sun.

Its open, flat roof in particular, which was littered with pots of shade-providing large-leafed palm trees, was almost idyllic. It was the perfect place to make the tedious business of washing and cataloguing all the finds from the previous day bearable, as each student and supervisor took a shift on cleaning and recording duty.

The suitability of the house at night was a different matter. With only Beth and Harrison's bedrooms having internal doors to close, and not many of the rooms having access to natural light, the very conditions that made the house a haven during the day caused it to be like a freezer by midnight.

Lying on her thin camping mattress, cuddling her sleeping bag and an additional blanket to her chest as if they were oversized teddy bears, Beth stared up at the cracked ceiling. For once the shabby nature of the room, with its concrete floor and grey-plastered walls, failed to radiate its inbuilt cold into her bones. Tonight, she was too incensed to notice that she was only protected from the permanently icy floor by an inch of inefficient padding. Her heart was beating too fast in her chest, and her palms and forehead felt sticky with the perspiration of hot embarrassment. Why? she asked herself. Why would Candida say those things about me?

Trying to block out the feeling that the happy laughter she could hear from the female students camped down in the next room was caused by her, a fully dressed Beth clambered into her sleeping bag. Plumping a pillow over her face, as much to keep herself warm as to adopt the ostrich mentality she knew would be the only way she'd be able to switch off enough to give her fatigued muscles some rest, Beth snuggled into as comfortable a position as she could manage.

Despite her efforts to clear her head, however, the details of what she and Ryan were alleged to have got up to on the open roof of the house tangoed provocatively around her imagination. She couldn't help but see the irony. How could Candida think she was going to convince anyone who'd actually met Beth that she could have exposed her sensitive flesh to the elements like that? She spent her whole life virtually buried in layers, be they protection against the sun, driving rain, or gusting winds. If her students had any idea how much Beth longed to be able to display her skin to the world, to have the kind of flesh that could be tanned without burning to a crisp in minutes despite being virtually drowned in lotion, then they'd dismiss Candida's claims as ludicrous.

Before she'd arrived in Africa, Beth had believed she'd be better off by covering herself in thin layers like the locals did. Now she knew different. There could be few things worse than shovelling sand all day in clothes that seemed to have been purpose built for getting grains stuck in the creases, and irritating the hell out of sensitive skin.

Thoroughly muddled as to how her ill-advised act of kindness towards Ryan had led to this suspicion of extreme fraternisation, Beth found herself fighting the urge to burst into tears.

Students had been developing unsuitable crushes on their supervisors since the first teacher had chalked on a blackboard; it was clichéd stuff. And you're just as bad! she admonished herself. Beth had always told herself that her admiration for Harrison was simply because his work was so good. In her heart she knew she'd been kidding herself. 'At your age you should not be getting crushes!'

Now she'd met Dr Harris, and he was nothing like she'd imagined, either physically or conversationally. And having made a total fool of herself in front of him, Beth knew it was time to make sure her crush was well and truly crushed.

But now he's kissed you, you aren't so sure, are you ... I wonder what the rest of his body tastes like?

Screwing up her eyes against the memory of his face, so close to hers that she could smell his masculine scent and feel quiet desire radiating from his body, Beth forced her mind to the problem in hand.

Until Harrison had said something, it hadn't occurred to her that Ryan had been acting like an over-enthusiastic white knight with any intension other than to make up for her for being such a clumsy idiot. But what if that wasn't it at all? she wondered. What if he does fancy me a bit?

The whole idea seemed preposterous. Beth cared so little for her appearance that she could go days without even a glance in the mirror. She was in the wrong sort of job to bother with decent clothes, she'd given up on finding make-up that didn't make her skin itch years ago, and her hair did what it liked, when it liked, and thus far no treatment had been invented to say otherwise.

The idea that a young Adonis like Ryan, who Beth had to concede was fit in every sense of the word, would want another, younger woman to think that he'd slept with her was mad – even if it was a little flattering.

Perhaps I should have just laughed off what Candida said when I was with Harrison? Even as she had the thought, Beth knew she couldn't have laughed. It had been a massive shock to discover someone was spreading such gossip about her. Trying to console herself with the fact that at least Candida's malicious conversation had been with someone on the other end of the phone and not someone on site, Beth wrapped herself up tighter, like a sausage roll in her insulated sleeping bag.

Eventually reaching a temperature which allowed her body to unclench enough to consider sleep, Beth's eyes began to droop. As the sheer exhaustion of her working day, combined with the conflicting emotions of the evening, sent her drifting toward unconsciousness, a treacherous voice at the back of her head asked whether she'd have felt so upset if it had been Harrison she was accused of having a kinky romp with.

I wonder what his dick feels like …

Beth awoke with a start and sat bolt upright. Her pulse was racing ten to the dozen. Flashes of the dream she'd been having replayed behind her eyes.

Harrison had been standing over her naked body, disappointed yet lustful craving etched on his face. He'd yelled at her, telling her she was a slut one minute, but then complaining he couldn't see her chest the next. Ryan lay on top of her, his bare back protecting her breasts from the sun as he gave her a blissfully slow fuck. The Beth of the dream was aware she wanted to speak, to make some sort of noise, but her mouth hadn't been able to open.

Shivering, Beth tried to take control of her night-time thoughts, clamping her legs together to deny her fast-growing arousal. She could almost feel the rough baked clay of the roof on her back, as she'd been trapped there in her dream. Ryan's thick cock had been moving rhythmically within her, his eyes focused on hers in such a way that Beth had been unable to look at Harrison to her left, or to the figure who silently stood to her right.

A fresh wave of clammy sweat trickled down a wide-awake Beth's neck. She hugged her sleeping bag to her chest as she realised who it had been standing with them in her dream. A supercilious Candida, an iPhone held out recording the salacious sight before her. The vision filled Beth with almost as much dread as if the dream had been a fixture of fact and not a figment of her imagination.

'This is utterly ridiculous!' Beth addressed the room in general as she wriggled out of her sleeping bag. Wrapping the blanket back around her shoulders immediately, she checked her watch. It was only half-past five in the morning. With a groan, she dug her toothbrush out of her bag, deciding that although extra sleep would have been most welcome, the dreams that might accompany it were not.

Creeping down the stairs as quietly as possible so she didn't wake anyone, Beth attacked her teeth, the simple act of hygiene making her feel better. With each brush back and forth she felt a little more awake, and her usual sensible perspective took charge of her out-of-control imagination.

These are the facts, she told herself as she rinsed the white paste around her mouth; first, you made an error of judgement over the mosaic. You've apologised, Harrison wasn't angry, and he isn't going to send you home, or report you for being an idiot. He respects you as an archaeologist. Second, Candida is a gossip. She probably invented the whole sex on the roof scenario so she'd have something to say to a friend in the States. Third, Harrison doesn't know you very well so you can't be too upset if he believed what he heard, especially after you withheld information about Ryan breaking the mosaic. And last of all, he kissed you because you were distressed and he was trying to calm you. He wasn't testing you out to see if you were a slut. But however nice it was, it meant nothing.

Beth spat into the bucket, rinsed it out, and poured the water away. All that remains, she continued to tell herself, is for me to say sorry to Harrison for overreacting, and to make sure that Ryan apologises for breaking the mosaic. Candida is Harrison's student and not mine, so her bad behaviour is his problem. Then perhaps I can get on with my job!

From the moment she'd been told she had got the job as co-supervisor on a world-class site with Harrison three months earlier, Beth had been determined to work as hard as she possibly could to prove her worth. Now, with her integrity questioned, she was more resolute than ever. No way would anyone get the impression she was even remotely unprofessional ever again. Deciding that going back to bed for only an hour was pointless, Beth headed towards the only room with furniture.

The dining room had one large table in it, with 12 chairs, each virtually jammed next to the walls; such was the limited amount of space.

'I made you a coffee.'

The voice coming out of the gloom of the poorly lit room made Beth jump a foot and give an involuntary shriek of surprise.

'Hell, doll! Are you *always* so jumpy?' Harrison, who looked as if he'd had very little sleep himself, sat cradling a chipped mug of what smelt to Beth like at least a triple, if not quadruple, espresso. He pushed a mug of a similarly rich milk-free concoction in her direction.

Dismissing the flutter between her thighs, as the need to feel Harrison's lips on hers grew again, Beth kept her tone light. 'What are you doing up?'

Sliding between a chair and the table so she could sit opposite him, Beth gestured towards the coffee that was far stronger than anything she usually touched. 'Thanks.'

Busily quashing the residue of his own erotic dreams of a naked Beth writhing on the roof of the house with his dick between her lips; images that had sent him wanking in the dingy toilet cubicle at two o'clock in the morning, Harrison merely said, 'I'm a terrible sleeper, especially when I have to sleep on freezing concrete. You?'

'I felt bad about how we left things last night.' Beth took a sip of her coffee and winced; it was pure caffeine. 'I'm sorry I overreacted. I'm not used to being suspected of sleeping with my students. '

Harrison held up a reassuring hand. 'I've been thinking about that too. Of course you were livid, and to be honest, after being accused of sleeping with someone in your charge I can't blame you. I totally understand. I mean, it's a basic rule. Don't sleep with people you work with, and definitely don't sleep with students in your care!'

'Even if they're of the musclebound Adonis variety, and owe you big time!' Beth risked a joke. She wasn't sure if it was the relief of finding that Harrison understood and had forgiven her uncharacteristic fury, or the coffee that was knocking her sense of humour back into place, loosening her up, but she was relieved to feel more like her normal self again.

A wry smile lit the corners of Harrison's lips. 'Even then!'

The way the green of Beth's eyes shone when she grinned back at him was doing unbidden things to Harrison's crotch, as he coerced his brain to revert to the business of the day. He gestured to the plans of the site. 'I've added in yesterday's finds and strata information. How does this look to you?' He knocked them towards Beth, who began to study the intricate, hand drawn work.

'How did you do this so neatly without a computer?' Beth's respect for her archaeological hero increased further as she ran a finger over the representation of the drainage ditch she'd found, and traced where she imagined it might run, until it met up with a similar system on the US side of the site.

'Practice. And a background in graphic design.'

'You were a graphic designer?'

'Briefly, once upon a time when the world was young.'

'I can't imagine you in an office.' Beth couldn't contain her surprise. 'In fact, I can't picture you being anything other than an archaeologist. You always seem to have been there! I was reading your books as I did my degree.' Then she added more shyly, 'You sort of influenced my decision about where to specialise.'

She could feel the blush starting before she'd

finished speaking, realising that she sounded a bit like a groupie.

Harrison laughed as he picked up his coffee. 'Thank you, doll, although I could do without being reminded how much older than you I am!'

'You aren't much older than me at all! I know you wrote *The Roman World in Archaeology* at an annoyingly early stage in your career. You make me feel like a total underachiever!'

'Doll, I wrote that ten years ago.' Harrison peered at Beth across the top of his mug, amazed at how difficult he was finding it not to reach out a hand to touch hers. 'I did two years as a graphic designer back in the States before I admitted to myself that, although it was a useful skill, my heart wasn't in it. I annoyed the hell out of my folks by changing my major at such a late stage in my degree.'

'No way!' Beth studied the plan again. She was curious about his past but, determined to remain doggedly professional, simply said, 'I guess we should get the grid set up in the middle of the site and join the two sides up.'

'We should also get a rota for a week of field-walking set up.' He produced a second drawing of the eight metre by eight olive field's layout, which was punctuated by nothing but a small hut he'd marked down on the edge of field three. 'I stayed last night and paced the groves.'

The easy manner that had flowed between them crumbled with the mention of the night before, and Beth shifted uneasily in her chair. 'I'm sorry you had to sort that out alone. If I hadn't been so thrown by Candida's lies I would have helped.'

'It's fine.' Harrison had been hoping they wouldn't have to discuss his hideous misjudgement of her again.

He was furious with himself for thinking that Beth would have anything to do with Ryan beyond teaching him, but she obviously wanted the air cleared. 'I'm sorry. I should never have believed Candida. Perhaps it would have been better not to tell you about it in the first place?'

Beth lifted the plans so she could examine them closer, and so Harrison wouldn't be able to see the desire she was sure was flashing in neon lights across her face as she battled not to reach across the table and kiss him. 'No, you had to tell me. It would have been far worse if I'd picked it up as rumour at the breakfast table. Anyway, it's my fault for not telling you about Ryan and the mosaic in the first place. Although I can't see what that has to do with Candida.'

'Nor can I. Either way, I should have dismissed her conversation as the fabricated gossip of a nasty young lady straight away. Very unprofessional of me.'

Beth's mouth fell open. It hadn't occurred to her that Harrison might consider his behaviour as unprofessional as she considered her own. Putting a conciliatory hand on his, feeling his warmth against her freezing skin, trying not to remember how good his flesh had felt when they'd shared their fleeting moment of intimacy the previous day, she said, 'You know we're in serious danger of going around in circles and beating ourselves up because two of our students behaved badly!'

Harrison chuckled. 'We are, aren't we? Hell doll, it has to be lack of sleep.' A wicked smile crept onto his lips, 'How about we give ourselves a treat? Time off from our two nightmare charges. Let's send Candida and Ryan on field-walking duty today. A few hours of them walking up and down olive grove fields, staring at the ground in the hope of spotting previously uncollected finds, should give them the day of tedium they deserve, you a break from the over-attention of Muscle Boy, and me a break from the trying charms of Miss Infection.'

Laughing properly as she downed the dregs of her coffee, Beth stood to go and confront the trauma of changing from yesterday's dirty clothes into today's soon to be dirty clothes. 'You do realise that Ryan and Candida will be Muscle Boy and Miss Infection to us from now on! We'll have to be really careful not to call them that in person.'

'True.' Harrison picked up his pen, ready to add more detail to his plans. 'I'd never really considered Candida as a disease before, but as she has been a pain in my side for ages, I think the nickname suits her perfectly.'

'Ages?' Beth halted in her walk toward the stairs. 'How come?'

'Ever since the first lecture I gave her class in her first year, she's had a thing about me. I don't think there is anything she hasn't tried to get extra attention. Arriving at my house uninvited, waiting for me in my car, making sure the world and his wife thinks we've slept together in many an inventive manner – which we haven't! The girl is shameless.' Without giving Beth the chance to respond, he added, 'You'd better get ready for the day, doll; the others will be up soon. I'll finish this.'

Feeling dismissed, Beth headed to her room, her head full of only one thought now. If Candida is such a pain in the butt, why did Harrison let her come on the dig in the first place?

Chapter Five

'Is it me, or has this morning been refreshingly relaxing?' Harrison held his hand out to Beth, helping to pull her from her knees to her feet.

Brushing the sand from her trousers, Beth grinned back at him. 'Bliss.' She almost added that it had been particularly nice to work without the knowledge that Ryan wasn't eyeing up her backside, but decided not to. Whispering so the other students couldn't hear her paranoia, she added, 'Any additional gossip about what you overheard yesterday?'

'Nothing. Apart from the odd chuckle about your dislike of snakes, today's chatter has all been at the "how cute is Bruce Willis now he's older and has shaved his head?" level.'

'Honestly! As if that issue was ever in doubt. Willis has a twinkle in his eye. The amount of hair on top of his head is neither here nor there. The man may not be the best looker, but he is hot. End of story.'

Harrison shook his head, affection plastered over his face. 'Did I tell you I think you're nuts?'

'Several times.' Beth stored away her companion's affectionate expression in her heart for consideration later on. Removing her hat, she gave her hair a few moments' fresh air, unwittingly making Harrison clench his fists together so he didn't reach out to caress one of the spiral tresses and bounce it through his fingers, before she rammed it back in place.

Signalling that it was time to break for lunch, and making sure the last student had disappeared from sight down the path towards the house before he spoke, Harrison said, 'How about you and I risk an ear-bashing from Miss Infection, and go and see how she and Muscle Boy are doing?'

Popping the fine bristled paintbrush she'd been gliding over some newly uncovered bricks into her pocket, Beth groaned, 'In this heat? It's a quarter to 12 already. I thought it was just us Brits who were supposed to be mad enough to go out in the midday sun?'

He put his hands on his hips in mock indignation. 'You wouldn't be using the weather as an excuse not to go and see our favourite students, would you?'

'Yes, I would. But I guess we ought to see how they're doing.' The smile was wiped from Beth's lips. 'Did you see Candida's face when I told her she would be field-walking with Ryan?'

Harrison grimaced. 'Sure did. I believe the word you're searching for is "acidic".'

Unscrewing the lid from the water bottle she'd had the pleasure of refilling for herself in Ryan's absence, Beth asked, 'I'm curious, did Candida ask you to alter the rota? I got the distinct impression that taking an instruction from me was tantamount to being forced to suck on a particularly bitter lemon.'

Harrison snorted as they walked; the description well suited Candida's entire demeanour when she'd come to him demanding that she field-walk with him, not Ryan. 'She did, doll.' Delving one of his large hands into his backpack, Harrison passed Beth a portion of sandwiches. 'Here, I didn't think we'd get time for lunch at the house.'

'Thanks, Harry. You're very kind.'

Stopping to hook his rucksack back into place, he fixed Beth with an unwavering stare, which was as playful as it was challenging. 'For the last time, my name *isn't* Harry.'

Fighting the instinct to blink, feeling the sheen of his eyes reflect off her own, Beth, fully aware of the hopeful stiffening of her nipples beneath her bra, spoke with equal determination. 'And my name *isn't* doll. I've told *you* before. When you stop calling me doll, I will stop calling you Harry.'

As Harrison continued to peer into her eyes, Beth's stomach knotted with desire, a desire she hoped he couldn't read from the light of her gaze. His voice was laced with a heavy edge of exasperation, as if he didn't really want to explain himself at all. 'I call you doll because you look like a doll. You're all china skin, cute features, and incredible hair. It's a compliment, woman! I, on the other hand, do *not* look like a Harry!'

Beth opened her mouth to retort that he was quite like Dirty Harry in a certain light, especially when he wore his hat tilted back, but thought better of it.

Harrison almost elaborated on his feelings but, sensible of how close he'd already come to breaking his "no more relationships with work colleagues" rule, took a bite from his sandwich. 'Oh for God's sake; it's fish again! I know we are lucky to have anything at all. But I swear Rosa can cook bread, couscous, fish, and nothing else.'

Beth took a mouthful of her own lunch, eyes sparkling as she chewed. 'She's a whizz with fish, all right.'

'But it all tastes the same. I can't even work out what sort of fish it is.'

'Stop moaning. We are lucky to have a cook, or even

food.'

'True.'

Beth risked a glance at him as they reached the other side of the village and the olive groves came into view. 'I got the impression you were going to say something else before you started eating?'

Harrison swallowed his mouthful of sandwich. 'I know it's given us a much-needed break, but I've been thinking that putting those two together alone for the day might not have been such a good idea.'

Beth, who'd reached the same conclusion only seconds after she'd seen Ryan and Candida walking off to the grove together, had been trying not to think about their potential mistake all morning. 'You could be right, but they seem to be getting on well. I'm pretty sure Candida's objections were because she doesn't like taking orders from me, not because she doesn't like Ryan. He obviously fancies her anyway. You only have to see the speculative way he looks at her. And anyway, for my sanity's sake it was essential. If I see Ryan leer at my backside once more I'll snap.'

'Can't really blame him for that, doll, you have a neat backside.'

Looking at Harrison in surprise as he delivered this additional compliment, Beth refrained from comment as they walked, wondering for the hundredth time if she should mention their kiss, but not wanting to be the one to bring the subject up in case he declared the whole episode a terrible mistake.

A few steps later, Harrison paused mid-stride. 'I don't think he fancies her. I'd lay money on Ryan having an agenda, though ...' Kicking at the dry soil with his walking boots, he added. 'I thought Candida might show off to Ryan while they were alone, and perhaps tell him who was on the other end of that phone call. If there is someone who thinks you should have an eye kept on you, I'd like to know who they are, wouldn't you?'

Backtracking over what he'd said, Beth frowned. It was all getting a bit surreal again. 'Hang on. What do you mean by Ryan "having an agenda"? If he's got a silly crush on me, I'm sure time with Candida will show him there are better, more available, things on offer in his own age bracket!'

Harrison couldn't believe someone so clever could so easily miss the obvious. 'You can't lack that much common sense, can you, doll? He fancies the ass off you. And if Candida has added that fact to her arsenal against you, and has used it to her advantage …'

Again, he didn't seem able to finish what he was saying. 'Come off it. Ryan's an adolescent with ideas about a bit of MILF. He's only been acting up towards me because he feels bad about the mosaic. I'm sorry Candida is such a pain in the arse for you, but if she's that awful, she shouldn't even be here. Why is she here anyway?'

Harrison dug his hands into his pockets. It was no good. He was going to have to tell Beth the whole story. 'Come into the shade a minute.'

Leading an apprehensive Beth into the shelter of a lone tree, Harrison glanced around to make sure that they weren't being observed, and drew her close to his side.

Outwardly managing to appear completely unaffected by his looming physical presence, Beth's heart rate tripled as the side of his body rubbed against her. The heady aroma from his leather hat mingled with the tinge of his workday sweat, taunting the inside her nostrils. Clasping her nails into her palms to sidetrack herself from the effect of her colleague's proximity,

Beth didn't dare look at him; consequently, she missed the grave pallor across his cheeks.

Registering how closed off Beth's body language had become, her eyes cast down, her arms ramrod straight at her sides, her feet planted next to each other, completely unmoving, Harrison felt as if he was side by side with a waxwork model. Scanning the landscape around them, he decided to get the worst of his revelation over with. 'How well do you know Linda?'

'Linda?' Of all the things Harrison might have been about to say, that was a question Beth hadn't seen coming. 'Not at all beyond workday hellos, meetings, and stuff. She mostly travels abroad, lectures the Masters students, and supervises the PhD guys. Until now, I just tutored the undergraduates and worked UK excavations. I've never been taught by her. I only joined the University of Wales two years ago as a post doc. Why?'

Reluctant to share his humiliation, Harrison knew he'd left himself no choice. 'Because I know Linda. Very well.'

The little amount of moisture in Beth's throat dried to dust. She'd been right in the first place. Harrison probably had sex with every woman he worked with. How foolish to hope she was special to him in some way. His compliments were just his way of softening her up before he dropped another bombshell.

Failing to conceal how hurt she felt, Beth said, 'Define "very well".'

'Shall we sit down? This could take a while.'

'We don't have "a while".' Beth spoke with pointed care. "We are here to work. The digging will restart soon, and we have a lot to do before then. We haven't even reached Ryan and Candida yet, so I'll remain standing if it's all the same to you.'

'As you like.' Leaning back against the trunk of the tree, Harrison sighed heavily through his next words. 'Linda first came to Tunisia with me two years ago.'

Wanting this conversation to be over with as quickly as possible, Beth interjected, 'Yes, I know. She was brilliant at what she did. So good, in fact, that your account of her work here, along with consistently glowing reports of her research, got her speedily promoted. I was shipped in to replace her at the grassroots level.'

'It wasn't that straightforward.'

'What the hell is?'

Harrison risked taking one of Beth's hands, and took courage from the fact she didn't immediately yank it away. 'Linda is a clever woman. Far cleverer than I'll ever be. We had a relationship while we were here, which continued as a highly flirty text and email relationship once we were back in our own countries.'

'Lucky you.' Beth could see it all very clearly. Linda's corn yellow hair swinging in plaits on each side of her sweetheart face as she body-bounced her colleague.

'Not so lucky, actually.' Swallowing his pride, he carried on. 'It was all a plan. A carefully worked out plot so that Linda could fast-track her way up the ladder. I was a convenient rung to assist her en route.'

Beth's eyes narrowed. She really wanted to believe him, and she knew it was true that Linda was incredibly ambitious, but she forced herself to remain sceptical.

'All the time I believed we had something, Linda was simply using my name and my connections to get on. When she asked for help, I gave it. But then I began to notice a pattern emerging. Papers I'd written that she had a junior authorship on slowly became papers that Linda had written herself, rather than pieces she'd merely contributed to. Digs I was advisor on suddenly became co-run affairs, or were taken over by Linda completely. I found out much later that she'd been contacting editors and grant bodies using my reference details, saying I was deferring to her time and time again.

'Each time she elbowed her way above me, Linda would laugh it off, making it sound like she'd had some good luck. With hindsight, I can see that when she felt a fraction of guilt she'd be all over me like a rash, thanking me for helping her so much. As Linda rose higher, my position became less dominant in the field. With each paper I lost to her, my own academic research rating slumped. I was so stupid. I didn't notice what she was doing at first.'

Harrison gaze landed on the small, fragile hand he was holding, distracting him from what he was saying. Beth was so slight. It was hard to believe she was as physically strong as he knew her to be, having seen her pushing a full wheelbarrow and wielding a pickaxe.

Noting the direction of his eyes, and not really understanding why she did it, Beth snaked her fingers through his, holding his palm properly. She found she was holding her breath, as she listened to her colleague.

'You must think me a fool. A sap, as they say on my side of the pond. The level of Linda's underhand manipulation astounds me as much as my own gullibility. Until I met her, all the archaeologists I'd ever met were kind, generous, and happy to share their knowledge. I was terribly naive. I made the mistake of thinking that just because she was young, pretty, and keen, she was a nice person.'

Edging a fraction closer to him – more, Beth told herself, to avoid the shafts of superheated light that were piercing her arm through the leaves of the tree and layers of her shirts as though she was being whipped with a well-aimed cat o' nine tails than because it felt good – she asked, 'Why are you telling me this? I'm sorry Linda screwed you over; but how is this relevant to our current situation? I came to Tunisia to do my dream job, and what I'm actually doing is being badmouthed by a girl with an overdeveloped sense of entitlement, and semi-stalked by one of my own students. Linda isn't here.'

'I'm telling you because I want you to understand that there is a reason why, despite the fact I desperately want to, I haven't kissed you again, I haven't told you that I find you fascinating, and would love to spend out of work time with you. I can't risk another relationship with a colleague, no matter how much I want to. And the reason I am telling you this *right now* is because Linda knows Candida.'

Beth threw his hand down and took a large step backwards as she tried to process the fact that he liked her. She wasn't going to act on that instinct at the same time as having to cope with more revelations about the busty blonde student who was spreading malicious gossip about her. 'Linda knows Candida?'

'Yes.' Harrison shoved his hands back into his pockets, fiddling with the trowel he kept in one, and a brush in the other, trying to deny to himself that his palms suddenly felt empty. 'And I've been thinking, what if Linda was the one on the other end of Candida's cell? What if she is using Miss Infection to check up on you? She never believed there was nothing in Candida's claims that I'd slept with her. If she believed I was two-timing her, this could be her revenge.'

The headache that was brewing thanks to the glare of midday was abruptly worsened by the hammering of renewed confusion in Beth's head. 'That all sounds like paranoia to me. Why would she? I'm nothing to do with Linda. She is a senior lecturer, and I've only just got my foot in the door academia wise. I am of no use to Linda *at all*. I don't have plans for supremacy like she does. This is what I love.' Beth jabbed finger at the countryside around her, and then, with a feeling of helplessness, tried to inject some humour and lighten the mood. 'Apart from the extreme heat and cold, of course. I can't see me falling in love with Africa.

'Look, Harrison, I adore ground level archaeology. I can't think of anything worse than climbing up the ivory tower of power, spending most of my working life in an office shuffling paperwork, and sucking up to people to try and extract dig money out of them. I want to be a real, dirty hands and muddy knees sort of an archaeologist.'

Harrison's head tilted to one side, his face a mixture of pride, relief, and lust. 'You do?'

'Well yes, of course.' Beth took a hefty draught from her water bottle. 'I want what I always wanted. I want to excavate the lost and make it found! I am *not* Linda. And trust me on this, once I am away from here, Candida will not be featuring on my Christmas card list.'

Turning abruptly, she looked directly into Harrison's eyes. 'To clarify the important part of this conversation, you fancy me, and – as you must have noticed – I like you too. But you're worried I'll screw you over like Linda did?'

'Not any more I'm not.' Harrison laid a hand on each of Beth's cheeks. 'I'm sorry I thought you could be like her for even a minute. I overheard Candida, and …'

Beth cut over his excuses. 'You seem to be saying sorry a lot for the assumptions you've made about me due to gossip in the last 24 hours.'

'I'm sorry.'

'There you go again.' Beth rose up on her tiptoes, and took hold of his rough-stubbled cheeks. 'Enough now. Enough.'

Harrison's lips hit Beth's on a mutual collision course of desperation to taste each other again. To experience a proper kiss, to wind his tongue around hers as his hands slipped to her chest, cupping her breasts through the layers of material which were insubstantial enough for him to easily determine the outline of her bra, was an experience he had, only moments ago, resigned himself never to have. Now it was happening, his cock was responding accordingly.

The high temperatures temporarily forgotten, Beth moaned yieldingly into his mouth. Unable to keep her hands to Harrison's face alone, reckless of the fact that they could be discovered by any passer-by, Beth eased her fingers down his front, feeling the bulge of his shaft beneath his shorts. All the images she'd had of what his dick would be like, what it might feel like, how it might taste, crowded into her psyche in one go. She needed to know now, before they found Candida, and she did or said something else to ruin things.

Deftly unzipping his fly, Beth slid a single fingertip into the gap, tickling his length though his boxers.

'Oh God, Beth.'

'Do you want me to stop?' Panting slightly as she spoke, Beth wasn't sure she could stop even if he asked her to as she sidled more fingers upwards, edging down the waistband of his underwear enough to get her palm wrapped around his length.

His penis sprang free easily, and as Beth cradled his pleasing weight in her fingers, Harrison's kisses became more savage, his stubble burning her, his hips thrusting forward.

All his intensions never to do this with Beth, let alone do it in an open space where anyone could walk past, dissolved in the sensations of her hold, which compressed and loosened over and over again, until he thought he'd explode in her grasp.

Hearing the adjustment in his breathing, Beth fell to her knees. She didn't wait for permission, but engulfed his length in her mouth, mewling with delight as Harrison rocked forward, filling her throat without gagging her.

Salty, sweaty, and yet sweet, Beth inhaled his delicious taste and texture as she sucked, driving him on, mindful of the lack of time, and desperate to see if his come was as flavoursome as she suspected it would be. For a second she held back, and smiled into his amazed eyes. 'I see you are hung like an *ass*, then!' Before refocusing on her work, inching herself nearer to him on her knees, she tucked another digit into his boxers, digging down so that she could stroke his backside as she worked him off. 'And your *arse* feels gorgeously taut as well!'

Half-laughing, half-stunned, Harrison stared in astonishment at the woman before him. Knocking her hat to the floor, he trailed his hands through her curls. Their softness, despite their constant exposure to sun and sand, was as smooth and satisfying as he'd dreamed they'd be.

Suddenly it was too much. The idea of what they were doing, and the fact it was Beth pleasuring him with extreme finesse, his penis deep within her throat, caused Harrison to act. With a stifled cry, he began to move with her. 'Doll, I can't hang on, I ...' Pumping twice against her mouth, his load cascaded from his cock.

Beth consumed the gloopy liquid in quick gulps, its creaminess soothing her parched throat. Then, business-like once more, she neatly wiped him off before popping his penis back inside his shorts. Peering up at him as she cleaned stray speaks of come from her chin with a tissue, Beth asked, 'So, do you think I am as slutty as Candida says now I've done that, or am I perhaps simply a girl who is rather keen on her co-supervisor, a man whose work I've respected for years? And who I have, despite my better judgement, got the serious hots for, *and* who, right now, I want very badly indeed. Which is a shame, because we have work to do. Now come on.'

'Linda said you were shy.'

'Linda said a lot of things.'

Harrison's mouth was still wide open in awe as Beth strode purposefully over the last few hundred yards to the olive groves. He wondered just how wet she was, and if her panties were damp for him. Who've you been kidding? he asked himself. This English chick isn't Linda. She's something a bit special.

Chapter Six

Resisting the temptation to cup her hand in Harrison's as they looked for the students who should have been in view already, Beth reverted to their conversation as if the previous few minutes hadn't happened. 'The thing is, I can't think of anyone who'd want to check on me, or who, if they heard what Candida had said down the phone, would believe them. Everyone at home, apart from Linda apparently, is lovely. And I don't know anyone on your side of the water, so I can't see how I could have upset them.'

'Exactly.' Harrison knocked back his Stetson as he spoke, showing a band of perspiration on his forehead. Not for the first time, he made Beth think of a movie cowboy. 'At first, I thought that maybe Candida had set me up. That she'd followed me to the garden, and there hadn't been anybody on the end of her cell at all.'

'Why would she do that?' Beth, her hands on her hips, stepped up onto the raised bank at the side of the field and scanned the olive grove, which was spookily devoid of human life. 'You said Candida spoke as if she was responding to someone on the end of the call, answering questions and stuff.'

Harrison sighed. 'She's quite the little actress, and I wouldn't put it past her to have invented the whole thing. However, the more I think about it, the more I'm sure there was someone there after all.'

Saddened by how quickly their moment of passion had been diluted by thoughts of Candida, Beth said, 'At the risk of repeating myself, why would Candida want to get you to believe that I am untrustworthy?'

Harrison spoke with inflexible deliberation. 'I told you, she is basically my stalker. She's been a pain in my butt for ages.' Harrison's voice lowered an octave as he gestured around them, to where he was expecting Ryan and Candida to appear any second.

'I can't see what Candida pretending to have slept with you has to do with her hating me!' Beth said, as he took hold of her hands.

Harrison snorted with a combination of exasperation and regret. ''Cos she feels threatened by you, of course.'

'What?' Beth spluttered against the mouth of her water bottle. 'That's stupid. She's younger than me, prettier than me, has a tan I would kill for, and a better body shape than mine by miles.'

Tilting the brim of his hat forward to shade his face, Harrison shut his eyes and took a deep breath. His annoyance at his student transformed into frustration at having to reassure Beth again; an act that seemed insane to him considering what she'd just done to him. 'I will say this once more, doll, so listen up. Candida is younger than you, but otherwise don't talk crap. You knock spots off her and you know it.' With barely a pause for breath he added, 'And the reason she is here is simple.'

'Simple?' Beth faltered. Had Harrison really just said that? Did he really think her more attractive than Miss Infection? Struggling to hold down her personal feelings, her mind travelled back over every conversation they'd shared since she'd arrived in Tunisia. 'Am I being really thick here or something?' Beth shook her head in bewilderment. 'How come

Linda's actually met Candida over here? This is a one-time dig for second year students only.'

'Usually it is, but Candida's an exception. She's a final year student, not a second year. This is her second visit to this site.' Harrison clawed a hand through his hair with the air of a man who'd had his fill of this particular student. 'I will tell you about it, although frankly I'd rather talk about that blowjob. Fuck, doll, you are *hot* at that! In the meantime, we must be getting within earshot if you see what I mean.' He lifted Beth's chin up, risking a quick kiss on her paper-dry lips.

Despite her body's desperation to draw him closer, Beth kept some distance. 'You'd bloody better.' Her cheeks were infused with two burning peaks, her pussy was too damp to ignore and her chest on fire. She felt awash with messy emotions she had no time to deal with. 'Where the hell are they?'

Harrison's frustration at their circular conversation twisted into anger at the stupidity of the whole situation as he barked, 'I have no fuckin' idea. Where did you tell Ryan to start the walk from?'

'Field one, the first we came to, then to progress north.' Beth looked at the map of the square grove area. 'Even if they were going way too fast, and have reached field three, we should at least be able to see them in the distance by now. This is why we should let them have mobile phones on site!'

'Doll, if Candida had her cell with her, *no* work would be done at all. Ever.' Harrison scowled. 'There isn't even any equipment lying about. Where are the measures, find trays, and stuff?'

As they stood on the dividing mound of earth the farmer had built up between the first and second field, a clammy trickle of foreboding oozed down Beth's spine. 'What the hell are they doing, and why have I got a horrible feeling that whatever it is has nothing to do with picking up shards of pottery?'

'It's quarter past 12. If they'd gone back to the house we'd have seen them pass us. If they have any sense they'll be sheltering from the sun for the next hour.' Harrison pointed into the distance. 'Maybe they packed up all the equipment and took it to the shack at the back of field three when it got too hot to work?'

Beth, trying not to speculate if their problem charges had walked past her and Harrison when they'd been otherwise engaged, was sceptical. There were no newly made holes in the crumbling earth to indicate that measuring posts had been pushed into the ground any time recently, and although Ryan might be a show-off, he was a good archaeologist when he wasn't pratting about. No way would he have missed the two large pieces of terracotta Samian ware she'd spotted only a few metres behind her.

'Well, whatever they're doing, it isn't working. Even if Candida has thrown a strop and persuaded Ryan to down tools, they have to be somewhere. That shack seems a good a place to hunt as any.'

'At least we'll be able to escape the sun for a moment.' Harrison's silent feet walked a little faster. 'I wasn't expecting to be out so long, I'm almost out of water.'

'Should I go back and check the others are OK?'

Not wanting Beth to leave him while the air of unresolved business hung in the air between them, and privately hoping they would enjoy some time alone in the hut, Harrison said, 'if we haven't found them by half-past 12, then we'll head back. We can trust the other students to act like adults without us.'

'OK, but let's stick to as much shade as we can. This climate is affecting my moods and judgement. I swear

I've never been so short-tempered or irrational in my whole life!'

Before he'd considered the consequences, Harrison asked, 'Is that why I got a blowjob then? You forget your common sense due to heat exhaustion?'

Beth stared at him, her smile not quite reaching her eyes as she tried not to be hurt by his comment. 'No, I did that because I wanted to.'

He watched Beth as she trudged on, her eyes fixed on the shack that belonged to the farmer who owned the groves. 'Did you know that when you blush your freckles get darker? The urge to trace my finger over your nose to join up the dots is huge.'

Glowing a richer crimson, Beth said nothing. Every time she thought she knew where she stood with Harrison, either professionally or personally, he threw some other revelation her way, be it good or bad. The idea of him tracing a fingertip over her skin wasn't helping her to keep the level head she knew she needed. 'Um, no, I didn't know that.'

The taste of him was lingering temptingly at the back of her throat, and no amount of water from her dwindling supply seemed to take the intoxicating texture and aroma of his shaft from her lips. Beth knew, however, that until she'd learnt more about what the hell Candida was up to, she mustn't let herself to be diverted by the pull at her groin or, more worrying still, the tug at her heart, which felt less like just a crush with every passing minute.

'There's no sign of them,' she said. 'So tell me, why *is* Candida here? I have to know now before my imagination fills in the blanks and makes things even worse than they are already.'

'The bottom line is she's here because her father is the head honcho of Harker International who, as you know, fund this dig. The only condition attached to the money was that Daddy's little princess comes here to work each season.'

'Seriously? Is that all? I was expecting something sinister after all this hassle!'

'That's all.' Harrison held out his hand beseechingly, 'Hey, doll, call me old-fashioned, but there's no one around to see us. Can I at least hold your hand, because being so near to you and not holding you is driving me nuts.'

As the humidity of the open fields wrapped around her, Beth squeezed his palm encouragingly, 'I'm glad you want to hold my hand. I want to hold you too. I want us to do a lot more, actually, but this has been a hell of a 48 hours. One minute I'm dreaming of what our bodies could do together, the next I'm accused of doing similar things with a student in my charge!'

Not sure whether to laugh or allow his imagination to run away with him, Harrison could barely breathe out his words. 'What sort of things do you want us to do together?' He gazed at his companion in avid awe.

'Apart from the fact that I intend to discover exactly how good it feels to have your dick inside me, you are not going to find out how far my fantasies about you stretch until we've found Muscle Boy and Miss Infection, and cleared this nonsense up once and for all. Are you sure there's nothing else I should know before we find them?'

Marvelling at the fact that Beth had been fantasising about him as much as he'd been dreaming about her, and wishing his brain wasn't so focused on his dick, Harrison braced himself. He knew he had to tell her about the final flourish to Candida's garden phone call. If he didn't, and she found out later, he'd lose Beth before he'd ever really got her, and that was a risk he didn't want to take.

'I've agonised over whether I should have told you this after I heard Candida's call. I didn't because I genuinely believed the last bit of her conversation was stupid gossip; an extra twist of nastiness to embellish her tale to whoever was on the end of the call. But, having seen how Muscle Boy behaves around you, and having got to know you better, I realise that I've got everything backwards. It wasn't the part about you having an affair with Ryan that I should have focused on – that was pure jealousy, I'm afraid. It was the other bit of her conversation.'

Beth suddenly felt as if she'd come down with a dose of 24-hour flu 'What other bit?'

'Promise you'll hear me out before you go completely nuts?'

'No.'

Sharply blowing out a lungful of sticky air, Harrison began to explain. 'Ryan has a bet on with someone back in the UK.'

Beth hardly wanted to ask. 'What kind of bet?'

'That he'll have sex with you before the dig's over.'

She felt herself blanch. 'I guess that explains a lot.'

Placing a finger gently over her lips, Harrison nodded. 'That's why he's been so attentive. The fact he hasn't been giving you room to breathe is nothing to do with his guilt over breaking of the mosaic. He did that deliberately so he could suck up to you. It wasn't an accident.'

The last remaining blood in Beth's face drained away. She felt faint, and for the first time in ages it was nothing to do with the scalding temperatures. 'I've been feeling like the whore of Babylon, and all this has been about is some juvenile bet!' Although she kept hold of his hand, her words could have cut ice as she demanded,

'You didn't think I should've been informed of this last night?'

'Sorry, doll. I almost told you, but I didn't want to make things worse than they were. If it helps, I honestly haven't heard any rumours about it amongst the kids.'

Unaware that she was clasping Harrison's hand so hard her nails were beginning to cut into his flesh, she mentally processed the implications of Candida's phone call and Ryan's bet. 'And what do you propose we do to sort this out?'

Harrison, not wanting to let go of her, even to escape the increasingly painful grip of her fingernails, clocked Beth's determined expression. It was time for action. 'First, we have to find them. Then you must find out if Candida has told Ryan what she's up to and why.'

'And how the hell do I do that?'

Harrison grimaced. 'You'll have to make Ryan think he has won his bet. You'll have to seduce him, and get the information out of him in the process.'

'You have *got* to be kidding.'

'And I –' Harrison drew himself up to his full height, his jaw set, his face grim '– will have to do the same with Miss Infection, because I'm willing to make a bet of my own. Whoever Candida is reporting to is the same person that Ryan is gambling with.'

'You think Linda's behind this mess, don't you?'

'Doll, this has got Linda's signature all over it.'

Chapter Seven

The old building had probably housed goats once, but now it was little more than a shelter from the worst ravages of the weather and a storage area for old tools. Its walls were intact, but cracks had opened in the dried-out wood, providing a plentiful range of spyholes should anyone wish to see within without necessarily being observed in return.

Each step they took across the groves towards the broken-down hut felt like making a move closer to insanity. The entirety of the past two days didn't seem to make any sense whatsoever to Beth, who forced herself to focus on the reality of the situation and not supposition. Come on woman, she told herself, you've got a brain. Work this out. Find a way to sort this without having to sell your soul to the devil.

Harrison thinks Candida is jealous because he likes me. Ryan is trying to seduce me because he has a bet on – which he is going to lose – and somehow Linda hopes to gain from this madness. So maybe ...

'Hang on.' The hut only metres ahead, Beth retreated a couple of steps. 'I've got an idea; one that might spare us from having to make the ultimate sacrifice.'

'Tell me.' Harrison's eyes darted around the vista as he listened.

'Why don't we use Candida's weapon against her?'

He tilted his head towards Beth. As she whispered

into his ear, a broad grin spread over his face. 'I take it all back, you're not nuts. You are brilliant!'

'It might not work.'

'I'd rather pretend to talk to Linda on the phone and "tell her everything" than have to pretend to be attracted to that harpy. And don't even ask how I was going to cope knowing you were coming on to Mr Adonis!'

Beth was about to say she'd had no intention of letting Ryan do more than think he was about to get his end away when a strangled murmur from the shack alerted them both. It was of such a pitch that it could only have come from Candida.

Indicating to Beth that she should stay where she was, Harrison moved closer to the building. Crouching, he peered through a crack in the wall, before inclining his head in Beth's direction. It was all the confirmation she required. She opened her mouth in surprise. A rush of vocalised hope that Candida and Ryan had got together after all, and would therefore leave her and Harrison alone, was stifled by the swift application of Harrison's hand over her mouth.

Quietly kneeling next to him, Beth peeped through another of the breaks in the once green-painted wood. This time, she clapped her own hand over her mouth to prevent the gasp that was hurtling up her throat.

Her mind reverted to what Harrison had overheard about how Candida couldn't imagine anyone begging another person for a fuck. She grinned to herself. Not so in control are we now, Miss Infection!

Ryan's back was to them; his denim shorts were in place, but his shirt was off. Any excuse to show off his pecs, Beth thought, knowing she shouldn't be watching, but finding it difficult to tear her eyes from the spectacle before them.

It wasn't the shapely muscles of her student's arms

or the smooth length of his back that held her attention, however; it was the girl on all fours behind him.

There was no chance Candida would see she was being observed, for Ryan's shirt was tied over her eyes, trapping her golden hair to the back of her neck. Her naked body was so still that only the slight swing of her breasts proved she was a real woman and not just an incredibly realistic sex toy.

Increased pressure around her hand bought Beth to her senses. Moving a few steps back from the wooden wall on tiptoes so as not to alert the students to their presence, she and Harrison regarded each other, mouths open in mutual shock. Already aroused by the blowjob she'd given him, Beth felt an extra tug at her crotch when she clocked the conflicting lustful emotions on Harrison's face.

Not wanting to risk being overheard by the occupants of the hut, Harrison took out his iPhone. Switching it to silent, he tapped urgently against the screen, before passing it to Beth to read. *Fuck! I know I shouldn't find that hot – but hell! Now what?*

Beth took the phone and typed her reply. *Stick to the plan. Wait until they're dressing, then we'll make a noise as if we've just arrived. Then u pretend to phone Linda.*

Glancing pointedly at his own groin, Harrison virtually ripped his cell from Beth's hands. *If we stay here watching that I am going to explode.*

Stifling the urge to giggle, Beth added to their silent correspondence. *If I can control myself, so can you. You're already a climax ahead of me!*

But we can't watch! They're our students.

I can. That girl has made the last 48 hours horrid. I want to see her grovel – and we might learn something if we listen to Ryan talking to her. U can go if u like.

65

If Beth thought she'd seen Harrison coloured with longing before, that paled into insignificance compared to the blaze in his steel blue eyes now. It was positively radioactive. Her insides contracted with a sharp jolt. It would have been so easy to haul him into the groves, to feel his cock slid inside her, giving her body what it craved so badly. But even her desperate desire to investigate every inch of him, to lick his torso and tease his shaft between her fingers, wasn't enough to outweigh her need to hear what Ryan and Candida might say to each other.

Taking hold of Harrison's hand, Beth steered him back to the hut. If she was going to risk her reputation by spying on her students, so could he. Sitting side by side on the dusty soil, she placed his hand on her breast, showing him in no uncertain terms how aroused on she was.

Harrison glanced at Beth with his eyebrows raised. Of all the things he'd had her down as a voyeur wasn't one of them. And yet, he thought as he felt the swell of her right breast poke a nipple into his fingers, *she is the girl who just gave me an incredible blowjob in the middle of a field ... They say it's always the quiet ones. So much for British reserve. I wonder exactly how unreserved she can be ...?*

The second the idea crossed his mind, he regretted it. The texture of Beth's lips as she'd manoeuvred his length around her mouth was an experience he'd never forget. Her tenderness, which had been undercut with a definite urgency, had left Harrison in no doubt that she wanted him for a lot more than a quick spot of oral.

As Beth's digits crept from his hand to his bent thigh, Harrison let go of the last hope that he hadn't been completely suckered by Linda, and finally accepted that her physical affections had only been perfunctory; not one ounce of emotion had been involved on her part.

Beth was regretting putting Harrison's hand over her tit as much as she was enjoying it being there. Even though a bra and two additional layers of cotton stood as a barricade between her bare flesh and his, the stealthy motion of his fingers over her nipple, repeatedly buffing its tip, was flooding craving through her chest, while her eyes remained fixed on the spectacle before them.

An unmoving Ryan towered over Candida, who he seemed to be torturing with inaction. As Beth watched, the throb of Harrison's pulse echoed from his leg through her palm and up into her pussy. The moans from Candida, which had been of the pleading without words variety, were beginning to increase in volume; suddenly, the moment that Beth was waiting for arrived as Candida's lipstick-smudged mouth yelled, 'Please, Ryan.'

His caressing Welsh accent responded more quietly, and Beth had to strain to hear what her student said as her own fingers walked to the base of Harrison's backside. 'Please, Ryan, what?'

'Please, Ryan, touch me! Do something!'

Mentally doing some calculations, Beth tried to guess how long Ryan had kept Candida in that position. If, as the amount of uncollected field scatter would suggest, they'd come straight to the shack that morning without doing any walking at all, it could have been for some hours. But how did he get her like this? Begrudging admiration for Ryan's seduction skills made Beth wonder if, should he have cranked the charm up a notch, it could have been her on all fours before him?

The idea of being there, air bouncing off her flesh, her chest hanging down, with a handsome naked man before her was not unappealing. But Ryan was the wrong handsome man. Beth's continuing line of reflection on the sheer bizarreness of the last few days was finally making her think clearly for the first time in what felt like weeks. Hang on a minute, she thought. Ryan had the chance to try it on with me. We spent a day on the roof together. Although he was flirty, he never went too far. Is his heart in this bet …? Is there even a bet at all?

As Harrison's hand continued to massage her nipple, Beth's imagination transposed the couple before them with herself and her companion; a scenario which caused every sensual fibre in her body to rush headlong to her groin.

She badly wanted to study Harrison's face; to see if the vision of Candida naked was having as much effect on him as it was on her. But Beth didn't look. She didn't want to risk missing anything as Candida yelled. 'Touch me, damn it!'

'Not until you agree to tell everyone the truth!'

Every hair on Beth's body stood up. This time she did look at Harrison. The expression on his face coincided exactly with what she was thinking. Which truth?

'Still not talking? OK.' Ryan took his mobile from his pocket. 'I think some insurance would be a good idea don't you?'

As the camera on his phone clicked, Ryan moved around the swaying body. Beth barely dared breathe, not wanting to alert her student to their presence.

'What the hell do you think you are doing?'

Candida's head swung from side to side as Ryan responded in soothing tones, 'Come now, Candida, I thought you'd approve of me having evidence of all the rumours I intend to spread about you. That's how you work, isn't it? And if there isn't evidence to be gathered, then you create some.'

Putting the phone away, Ryan sat cross-legged in front of his captive's bowed head. 'Now then, honey, you were telling me earlier that Beth and I were having an affair?'

'Only because you said you were!'

Ryan shook his head. 'And why do you think I said that? Do you think I might have made it up? A lie down an empty telephone line to see if you were listening in on other people's private conversations, perhaps?'

'But ...'

'Didn't you think it odd that the other students aren't talking about it? You've been on enough digs to know that few groups of people can gossip like archaeologists facing a landscape of mud or sand.'

Ryan moved to Candida's side, dancing a single finger up and down her slender spine. 'Just say if you'd like me to stop touching you, honey. I would hate you to accuse me of acting improperly.' He lifted his hand away. 'Shall I stop, Candida?'

Beth could feel the knot of tension bunch in her throat with the effort of not prompting the conversation in the hut. Ryan, it seemed, had decided to trap Candida with a fake call, just as she and Harrison had planned to.

Another two seconds passed before Candida spoke, her famously loud voice muted to a humiliated squeak. 'Touch me, Ryan. Please. I'll explain if you do.'

'Certainly.' Shuffling around to her backside, Ryan stood facing the wall that Harrison and Beth were peering through.

As one, the supervisors retreated a fraction, but not so far that they couldn't see or hear how his hand outlined the petite round of the nude buttocks. 'I'm glad. You have a beautiful posterior, Candida. I've wanted to touch it for some time. I must repeat, however, that if you wish me to give you the fucking you so obviously want, then a full explanation had better be forthcoming.'

A sharp gasp shot from Candida's mouth as Ryan's hand disappeared from view, making Beth suspect he'd just inserted a finger in or around her pussy.

'You have a magnificently tight little hole, honey. And so wet! Are you sure Beth is the one who's a slut and not you? Because the evidence here seems to be to the contrary! And, as archaeologists, we should always take the evidence of our eyes *very* seriously, don't you think?'

Beth knew she was in real danger of screaming in frustration as Harrison's hand continued to move over her clothes, but not beneath them. She needed to feel him directly upon her skin. Now.

Not averting her eyes from the scene before her, Beth grabbed Harrison's hand, pulled up both the tops she wore, and manhandled his unresisting palm up inside. Biting into the insides of her cheeks to prevent a groan of ecstasy as he flipped down the cup of her bra and clasped her pliant flesh, Beth replied by fondling his buried cock through the material of his shorts.

Still they watched, like rabbits caught in the headlights of sexual craving, the wrongness of watching outweighing the need to hear what was said.

Ryan was stroking Candida's rump now, 'Honey, I think you should talk, don't you? I mean, I would put money on Beth or Harrison turning up to find out why the hell we haven't done any work this morning fairly soon.'

'But they don't know we're here!'

'For fuck's sake, Candida! Where else could we be if we aren't in the fields, at the house, or on site? Think, woman. I know damn well you are intelligent, so use that brain of yours and work out what's best. I could easily walk out of here now, complete with my nice new photographs of you, and leave you horny and desperate.'

Candida growled, 'You want me too much for that!'

'Don't kid yourself, honey. Yes, I'm stiff for you. You're bloody hot, and if you'd just stop all the stalker informer crap, then I'll admit I'd like to have serious fun with you! In the meantime, what's to stop me wanking off over your body and heading off to collect pottery without you? Nothing at all.'

Beth frowned. She couldn't understand why Candida didn't just stand up.

Risking edging forwards a bit, hoping that Ryan was too intent upon his comrade to notice any alteration in the shadows, Beth rose up on her knees, and peered through a higher crack in the wood to get her first view of the dirty floor, and Candida's hands and feet.

The tape measures, which should have been lined up in the fields to mark off any major discoveries in the olive groves, were looped around her hands and feet, joining all four of Candida's limbs together in an elaborate figure of eight. Although it wouldn't have been impossible for her to escape, it would have been difficult.

The conversation in the hut had stopped.

A minute passed.

Nobody moved. Nobody spoke.

Then Beth felt her insides somersault as Ryan licked the finger he'd obviously been paddling in the juices escaping from Candida's channel. 'You taste delicious. Shame I won't be getting my mouth between your legs for a proper feast. Still, as I say, it's your choice.' He came back to Candida's head. 'I guess I'll just bring myself off then. Shame.'

'Wait!' A long sigh issued from Candida's lips. 'You know I could have got out of here ages ago, don't you?'

'Yes, but you are still here. And you let me tie you and bind your eyes.' Ryan sat down again, his hand lifting her chin.

'Why do you think I let you?' Candida's voice was faint, the edge that could take varnish off woodwork gone.

'I assumed you hoped I'd leave and Dr Harris would find you. I've seen the way you look at him sometimes.'

'No!' Candida sounded genuinely indignant, hesitating only slightly before adding, 'It's because this is what I like.'

Ryan snorted out a sharp laugh, 'A submissive? You? Now that I hadn't seen coming.'

'Linda saw it, though. Linda sees everything. I swear the woman has extra-sensory perception.'

'I think she's just a nosy bitch who is frighteningly ambitious, but you may be right. So this is what you want Harrison to do to you?'

'Not any more, not since Linda told me she was his girlfriend.'

'Linda and Dr Harris? Blimey!' Ryan stroked her hair as it shrouded her shoulders. 'Well, honey, if he ever did have designs on you, you siding with the slanderous Linda will have killed that off. I assume she fully believes that you and Harrison are an item?'

'Yes. And that's the problem.'

Ryan lifted Candida's chin and kissed her full on the mouth, before drawing back. 'I don't understand you. You're smart, cute, and from what I've seen when you do work, you're a good archaeologist. Why waste your time being such a bitch to Beth?'

'Linda. When I was here before, well, I had sort of made it known that I liked Dr Harris – and that we, um, went out and stuff. She totally bought my stupid claims about having a fling with him, and of course she knows my father.'

'Your father?'

'He's loaded, and old-fashioned and, worst of all, he funds this dig. Linda threatened to tell him that I was sleeping with Dr Harris if I didn't rubbish Beth. Dad would have gone crazy and taken me off the course. He'd also have stopped funding the excavation.'

Ryan let out a whistle of understanding. 'So Linda was blackmailing you with your own lies. And I guess if you suddenly admitted you'd lied about having a relationship with Dr Harris after you'd spent so long saying you had, hardly anyone would believe you, and you'd look a fool into the bargain.

'But if Linda told your father, who presumably would have tried to kill Harrison as well as withdrawing the funding for this excavation, the scandal would have been huge, and Harrison would have lost his job? Wow! Complicated! That Linda is a piece of work!'

'I've been an idiot.'

'Yes, you have, especially as there are plenty of younger men who'd be quite happy to give you exactly what you're after.' Ryan kissed her again, ripping off Candida's shirt blindfold. 'Although not many of us would be prepared to take the time to see if you were a nicer person than you pretend to be!'

'Would you?' The hope in Candida's voice made Beth feel sorry for her for the first time. She'd been naive and manipulated by Linda, just like Harrison before her.

'Are you sorry for what you did to Dr Andrews?'

'Linda told me that Beth had a history of seducing her male students. She said I wasn't to be conned by her sweeter than sweet look. When I saw her in your lap after the snake scared her, it looked as if what Linda had said was true.'

'What a load of crap! Beth's a bit of a flirt sometimes, but only in fun. Seems Linda just wanted to make ultra-sure you didn't like her. God knows why, though.' Ryan planted another kiss on Candida's lips, 'Will you say sorry to Beth?'

'Linda thinks Dr Andrews is too good at her job for her liking. You can guess the rest.' Candida shut her eyes for a second, before opening them wide, their blue irises shining. 'And yes, I'll say sorry.'

'Then in answer to your earlier question, yes, I would like to find out how nice you really are.' Ryan began to undo the ties at Candida's feet and hands. 'Get yourself dressed. Apologise to the bosses. Act like the decent human being I'm sure you are underneath, and I promise that, if you want me to, I'll treat you exactly like the naughty little girl you are very soon. But first, I'd like to get to know you better. Dinner in Sousse on our day off?'

Beth and Harrison silently walked a few paces away from the hut. For once, it wasn't just Beth's complexion that was pale. She was about to break the silence when Harrison wrapped her in his arms, the tension that had been caused by Linda's manipulations sliding from his shoulders as he bought his lips to hers.

Lost in his kiss, her hands wove up inside his T-shirt, sighing in surprise at the unexpected spring of his lightly haired chest.

A sudden vibrating from his cell phone made Harrison hurriedly step back. It seemed it had been Ryan and not Candida who'd broken the no mobiles on site rule. He'd sent Harrison a text.

You can both come in now.

Chapter Eight

'Candida has something she'd like to say to you.'

'She isn't a child, Ryan.' Harrison shot the Welshman a warning glance as he surveyed the interior of the hut. A pile of field-walking equipment and tangled tape measures was heaped on the grubby floor. 'She can say sorry all on her own. In the meanwhile, perhaps you could both explain how you're going to get a whole day's work done in one afternoon?'

Beth's eyebrow's rose. In her desperation to find out what had been behind Candida's malicious lies, not to mention her pussy's constant reminders that she felt as horny as hell, she'd temporarily forgotten about the work they were supposed to be doing. Glancing at her watch, she saw it was almost one o'clock. The other students would be wondering where on earth they'd got to.

Candida, her usual haughty disposition somewhat diminished, stood with as much dignity as she could muster. 'You were watching?'

Harrison virtually growled, 'Neither of you was where you should have been. We were worried that something had happened to you.'

Beth didn't trust herself to speak. The image of the American on her hands and knees remained vivid in her head, and the seat of her own panties was sodden with the prospect of what might happen when she and

Harrison were finally alone. The kiss she'd exchanged with her co-supervisor lingered like a future promise on her lips, helping to absolve the adolescent mistakes of the young woman before them. Suddenly, they just didn't seem worth the worry they'd caused.

'How dare ...'

'Candida!' Harrison cut across her, his entire body bridling with barely suppressed irritation. 'Don't you even *think* about judging us. We had no choice but to watch if we wanted to learn who you've been spreading lies about Beth to.'

His student took a step back in surprise at Harrison's rarely unleashed fury, her hand going out to Ryan's for support. Ryan took it, but his eyes never left Beth, who stared back at him, searching her student's features for some sort of comprehension as to why he'd been so keen to defend her honour in the first place, and in such an elaborate way.

Candida's voice ricocheted off the thin walls at full volume. 'What? I could report you! You – you saw me ... Like that!'

'For heaven's sake, Candida!' Harrison snapped. 'The entire campus of Colorado thinks I've already seen you like that, thanks to your rumours! What you've done to me is bad enough – I mean, what other university would touch me now, thinking I was having an inappropriate relationship with one of my students – but I'll be damned if you're going to do the same thing to Beth.'

Candida, knowing she was in the wrong, reverted to her more familiar scolded child look. 'Students do go out with lecturers sometimes,' she pouted.

'Yes, but they do *not* shout it from the rooftops.' Harrison ripped his Stetson from his head. 'Don't you see, Candida? University rules are very clear.

Relationships between students and staff are severely disapproved of. If it does happen, then the lecturer is pointedly advised to seek work elsewhere. The only reason I kept my job, after all your lies, is that the Vice-Chancellor is a friend of mine, and doesn't believe a word of it. Plus, of course, he didn't want to upset your father. Money, I am reluctant to say, talks!'

Candida's tanned cheeks shone a brighter red, and her mouth opened and closed like a goldfish gasping for air, as Harrison asked, 'Why didn't you simply tell us the truth about Linda? About the blackmail? I would have helped you!'

Beth could almost feel the adrenalin pumping through Harrison's veins as he fought to regain his usual quiet state. He gestured to Ryan with his head. 'Unlike this young man here, I am not your type, Candida. You must have realised that, surely? I don't have so much of an inflated ego to believe that your crush on me could have lasted for more than a week or two.'

Candida reddened further as she confessed, 'I did like you. A lot. For over a year, actually. And I really wanted us to – you know. But by the time we got here again, and I saw you getting on so well with Beth, I realised it had worn off. But the rumours I'd begun got out of hand, and of course Linda had picked up on the site gossip last year. She was livid. I hadn't realised she was with you at the time.'

'So –' Beth took a sip from her water bottle '– Linda stored up your lies until they could be useful to her. I presume she told you that your father would be informed of your slutty behaviour if you didn't blacken my name.'

Tears prickled at the corner of Candida's eye, and she sniffed quietly. 'Linda called me three weeks ago. She said that …'

'Linda! Always freakin' Linda.' Harrison's roar cut through Candida's explanation. He addressed Beth. 'No wonder she referred to you as the "one to watch", doll. I didn't think she meant like this! She's a fuckin' maniac!'

'It's OK.' Beth flipped his hat out of his hand and stuck it back on his head.

'How on earth is this OK, doll?'

Beth raised herself onto her tiptoes and kissed the end of Harrison's nose, no longer caring that they were being observed. 'Because Linda just lost all her power.'

Candida's forehead wrinkled. 'How?'

'You are going to tell Linda that your father already knows about your now extinct obsession with Dr Harris, and that she forced you to use it as insurance against him ever revealing how she manipulated him to fast-track her own position. If you need to, you can say that you also intend to tell him that you've been rubbishing my name because she sees me as a rival to her own supremacy.'

Far from convinced, Candida added, 'Why would Linda believe me? And my father would go nuts!'

Beth smiled, finally seeing how absurdly complicated they'd all made this situation. 'Your father won't know.'

'But …?'

'For supposedly intelligent people, we haven't half been stupid here! Listen.' Beth held up her hand for silence. 'Now Linda has finished using Harrison as her gullible ladder to success –' Seeing Harrison wince, she added as an aside, 'Sorry, hon, but you were gullible. We are just left with her insecurities surrounding my rise through the university's ranks. A rise that exists only in her head.'

Beth sighed as Candida looked blank. 'Candida, if

you hadn't noticed, you are 22 years old! You don't need parental permission to live your life. Plus, this dig only has one more season left. Neither Wales nor Colorado Uni are going let the work that's already been done go to waste if your father decides to pull the plug on the funding. Which he won't, by the way, 'cos Linda will *never* tell him anything.'

'You sound very sure.' Ryan, his eyes shrewd, tilted his head to one side as he listened to his supervisor.

'All Candida has to do is tell Linda that her father knows everything anyway. Linda is hardly going to call him to ask, is she?'

Harrison laughed. 'I can picture it now!' Adopting a terrible high-pitched English accent, he tried to sound like his ex. 'Good day, Mr Harker, I was just checking to see if you'd heard how I conned Dr Harris and blackmailed your daughter?'

Candida was still unconvinced. 'I'm not sure I can talk to Linda. I'd crack under cross-examination!'

Ryan wrapped an arm around her waist. 'I could. Linda doesn't worry me, and as I have no plans to do any of her courses, she won't have any influence over my final degree mark.'

Beth nodded. 'You could, thanks, Ryan. First, though, can I ask why you set Candida up like that? In that way, I mean? You could have just asked her outright what she was playing at.'

'You mean apart from the fact I fancy the pants off her?'

'Apart from that.'

'Isn't it obvious?'

'No.' Harrison and Beth spoke in unison, impatient for an answer.

'Candida's not exactly quiet. I overheard her on the phone to Linda. And what I learnt didn't square with the sort of things the nice American girl I'd got to know on site over the past week would say.'

Harrison nodded. 'The same call I overheard about you and Beth on the roof and your bet?'

'No.' Ryan grimaced. 'I did hear that call, but it was an earlier one that made me suspicious. I wanted to know why this cute Yank was rubbishing my boss in such a nasty way. I knew it was Linda at the other end. I could hear her shouting down the phone. That's when I decided to discover exactly what Candida was reporting to Linda by telling her I'd broken the mosaic in order to trick a fuck out of Dr Andrews. To make sure Candida fell for my lie, I made sure she heard me make a fake call.

'I kept an eye on Candida after that. Then I saw her making a call to Linda in the garden too. If I'd seen you, Dr Harris, I would have spoken to you sooner.' Ryan focused on Candida's deathly white face as he spoke, his eyes trying to reassure her that everything was OK now. 'I knew she was talking a load of crap about Beth better than anyone. I'm darn sure I'd remember if someone as gorgeous as Beth decided to seduce me. I didn't like the idea of other people hearing such gossip. And anyway, after breaking the mosaic I figured I owed her big time.'

Ryan addressed Harrison. 'I'm sorry about the mosaic. It really was an accident. I was being a prat. I've been trying to make it up to Beth ever since.'

Surprised at the strength of his relief that Ryan hadn't broken the mosaic as a backhanded way of getting into his supervisor's knickers, Harrison nodded.

'Apology accepted, Ryan. Although I would advise choosing a simpler way of making amends next time!' Taking hold of Beth's hands, he smiled. 'Well then, I guess we should all get back to work, unless you have any other bright ideas, doll?'

Grinning up at him, her eyes gleaming with kinky promise, Beth answered, 'I have lots of ideas, actually, but let's get this sorted once and for all first!'

Trying to ignore the effect Beth's flirting had on his body; Harrison said nothing as she took out her phone. 'Here you go, Ryan. This is Linda's direct office number. Call her.'

Chapter Nine

'How was Sousse?' Beth stacked away the last of the find trays and ran a critical eye over the deserted bath house site.

'Fine, thanks.' Harrison bent over the mosaic at their feet, habit making him brush it gently with the brush he kept in his pocket. 'Sorry I was so long. It took ages to find what Rosa asked me to buy for her. Have you been OK here?'

'Great.' Beth passed him the daily report sheets. 'The teams have worked well this afternoon, and apart from being half a day behind with the field-walking, we are up to speed.'

Harrison smiled, but seemed distracted as he studied the sheets detailing finds of beautiful beads and a broken strigil in his hand without really seeing them.

'You OK?' Beth knelt so she was at eye level with him. 'You should be beaming from ear to ear. You aren't going to be bothered by Linda any more. We played into her hands by reacting to her. No more overreacting means no more trouble.'

'What about you though, doll?' He looked worried. 'She could make your life miserable when you get back.'

'She could try; but as I'm not interested in going beyond the level of doctor, I can't see why I'm worth her energy.' Rocking back on her haunches, Beth pocketed her own brush. 'I still don't get why Linda was so worried about me. I'm no threat to her at all.'

'All I can think is that her guilt at how she climbed so high so fast has made her paranoid.'

'You think she was worried you'd tell me more about her ascent to power than she'd want me to know?'

'Ironically, if she hadn't tried to manipulate things via Candida, I wouldn't have said a word. I'm not exactly proud of being such an idiot where she was concerned.'

Beth placed a warm hand on his bare knee. 'Well, according to Ryan, Linda barely said a word in response to his call. Stunned silence is all he got, and an occasional squeak of agreement to his demands that we all be left alone. I've a feeling she'll give me a wide berth rather than confront me.'

'Well, there is another option.'

'There is?'

'I called Colorado while I was in Sousse. There's a vacancy in the department. What do you think? A bit of a change from the Welsh rain.'

Beth flicked her eyes up to his. 'Seriously? You want me to work with you?'

'You English! You always ask such stupid questions!'

Beth tilted her head to one side. 'Can I think it over?'

'Sure.'

Feeling dizzy from too much sun, Beth rose back to her feet. 'I think I should eat before I have to cope with anything else today. Come on, it's time to tackle some of Rosa's unspecified fish!'

'Well, actually –' Harrison slipped his hand into hers '– I thought perhaps you'd like a change from the fish and couscous diet.'

'How?'

Harrison's lips raised in a suggestive smirk. 'You'll see, but first I think it's time we took advantage of the fact it's my evening to use that trickle of water that laughingly calls itself a shower.'

The lust that had subsided from a full-on blazing blast to a simmering heat of happy expectancy inside Beth as she'd worked bolted to the surface. 'But the students …'

'Are all about to eat and, thanks to my trip to Sousse, enjoy a heap of local delicacies that are in no way fish-related. They'll not be leaving the dining room for a while.'

Keeping up with Harrison's silent stride, Beth felt the tingle at her pussy increase when he said, 'Did you know that you are the only one on this entire site whose knees I haven't seen?'

Beth laughed. 'I fear they are not my best feature.'

'You mean despite being covered all the time, they are covered in bruises and scars from all the kneeling you have to do when you're digging deep.'

'Yep.'

'That is my very favourite type of knee.'

Harrison steered Beth up to the very top of the house, where the shower cubicle took up one small corner of the open roof. Shrouded by some well-placed pot plants, and a rigged-up shower curtain, a sheet of corrugated metal balanced over its top protected the user from the worst of the sun or chill of night.

'Wait a minute –' Beth pointed toward her room '– I need a towel and stuff.'

'No, you don't.'

Beth couldn't believe it. The rooftop had been swept clean of its usual fine silt of sand, and all the detritus of cleaning and recording the collected artefacts was piled neatly along one wall.

Next to the shower were two brand new fluffy towels and a thick picnic rug, which had been neatly laid out, with a bag of food and drink propped next to it.

'This is incredible! How did you do this without anyone seeing?'

'Ryan and Candida.' Harrison twisted Beth gently at the shoulders so she was facing him. 'I figured we had no secrets from them now, and as they seriously owe us a favour, they kept everyone away.'

'How?'

'No idea, and frankly, my dear ...'

Beth burst out laughing. 'Let me guess. You don't give a damn?'

'You got it, doll.' As Harrison's arms wrapped around her, all the bubbles of uncertainty and desire that had been cartwheeling inside Beth over the past few days collided with the fantasies she'd harboured about Dr Harrison Harris ever since she'd first read his book all those years ago, and exploded in the pit of her stomach. She felt like a groupie whose dream of dating her favourite rock star had come true.

Her head swam as Harrison, his methodical pace both gorgeously sensual and frustratingly slow, extracted the layers of cotton from her belted waist. As the first graze of a fingertip met Beth's hips, she began to give as well as she got. Gripping the bottom of his shirt, Beth yanked it up over his head. Her palms swept over his torso, the rush of pleasure at feeling his taut flesh, gritty with sand, like a supercharged aphrodisiac.

Harrison, his breathing rapid, his lungs feeling as if they were only capable of coping with tiny amounts of air at a time, took hold of Beth's long-sleeved shirts, and returned the favour.

The chilled evening air that played around their semi-naked bodies went unheeded as the two archaeologists devoured each other with their eyes, their hands moving with equal enquiry over each other. Harrison only stopped the progress of his fingers when he reached the outskirts of Beth's faded green bra.

Beth's throat snagged as her partner placed the flats of his hands over each cotton-covered globe. The pressure was far less than during the tense moments of listening outside the hut, yet a million times more arousing. A mewl escaped her mouth, but otherwise she found it impossible to speak as her nipples fought back, the swell of her chest filling every millimetre of her underwear.

She found herself thinking she ought to do something, say something, move faster, but nothing existed in that second but the feel of his hands. When Harrison finally reached around and undid the clasp of her bra, Beth let out a massive exhalation of oxygen she hadn't realised she'd been holding in.

Harrison's pupils dilated wider than ever. 'They're even on your tits!'

'I'm sorry?' Beth peered downwards, expecting to see trapped sand or dirt or, worse, day-old spilt couscous smeared against her chest, but there was nothing there.

'Freckles. You have freckles on your chest.'

Instantly self-conscious, Beth went to fold her arms over her breasts, but Harrison batted them away. 'Oh no you don't, doll. I've waited ages to see how far those little beauties go, and you aren't going to cover up a single one.' Bringing his face in for a detailed examination of her skin, which was beginning to add goosepimples to its dotty collection, he began to lick Beth's flesh, the very tip of his tongue joining the generally spattered freckles together.

'Oh my God ... I ...' Liquid gathered at Beth's nub

as her chest received the most loving worship it had ever experienced. Her hands held Harrison's shoulders as he lowered himself to his knees so his tongue could meander around the underside of her chest.

Dropping a hand, Harrison undid Beth's belt, clumsily shoving her trousers past her hips. When he lifted a hand to cup the crotch of her panties, she couldn't hold back. Ever since she'd tasted his length in the olive groves she'd been fantasising about how it would feel if he caressed her between the legs. Now his hand was there, with only a thin strip of fabric separating his flesh from her mound. Beth cried out, 'Harrison, oh fuck …' She spoke through clenched teeth, 'I-if you don't stop I'm going to come … I … Oh God …'

Instead of slowing, Harrison clenched his hand open and closed, his tongue waltzing up over the round of her right breast.

Beth shuffled nearer, craving more pressure as he fixed his teeth around her nipple, flicking his tongue over the end so rapidly that the sensations engendered tipped her towards a climax. Dragging her knickers down, Harrison dug a single finger deep inside her, while his thumb copied the gesture of his tongue over her clit.

All Beth's intensions to enjoy the build-up for as long as possible evaporated as her orgasm crashed through her. She slumped forward, her ability to support her own weight impaired by the rainbow of erotic delirium that splashed behind her closed eyelids.

As his lover rested on his shoulder, Harrison eased himself into a sitting position, and tucked Beth onto his lap, his fingers stroking her russet ringlets, his words heavy with unspent lust. 'You OK, doll?'

'Umm.' Beth felt as if her voice was coming from far

away as she replied, the presence of Harrison's solid cock digging into the small of her back, keeping her pussy hungry and slick as she reached up to kiss him.

'Time for that shower, I think.' Harrison assisted Beth to her feet, levering the tangled jeans and panties that had fallen to her ankles.

It didn't matter that the water coming from the showerhead was more of a trickle than a cascade, or that its temperature was tepid at best. All that mattered to Beth was that she wasn't in there alone.

She was just thinking she could happily stand and admire his nakedness all day when Harrison hopped out of the cubicle. 'Stay there; keep warm under the water.'

'Where are you going?' Beth watched as he streaked across the roof to their clothes. His back seemed broader than she'd imagined, and although she knew he was very fit, the reality of his naked physique almost took her breath away.

She gulped, her whole being giving a lurch as Harrison waved a small, thinly bristled finds brush in her direction. 'Now, what sort of archaeologist would I be –' he stepped back into the small cubicle '– if I didn't have the correct equipment ready when it came to surveying a particularly magnificent specimen?'

Beth's mouth fell open as he knelt awkwardly in the confided space.

'Now, let me see your knees.' The light bristles of the brush she'd seen being so delicately swept over the mosaic earlier wiped over her kneecaps. 'Oh wow!'

The water barely reached Harrison as he ran the brush over the backs of Beth's knees, while kissing and licking her patellas. Beth couldn't keep her feet still. No one had ever treated her knees like an erogenous zone before, and her whole being squirmed.

By the time his investigation of her spotted skin had

reached above her knees, Beth was quivering with cold as well as desire. Water droplets were suspended from the tips of her breasts; trickling in tiny brooks on a course towards the V of her pussy.

Harrison could tell it wouldn't take much more to tip Beth over the edge; but she was also getting very cold. 'This investigation will resume very soon, but first –' he picked Beth up and laid her on the picnic rug '– let's make sure you don't freeze to death.'

Taking a towel, he began to dry Beth down, each rub enflaming her flesh further. As he worked, Harrison gestured to the bag of food to their side. 'You hungry?'

'Very.' Beth, whose knees felt oddly neglected, pulled her fellow archaeologist down on top of her. 'But not for food.' Haphazardly tugging the towel from between them, she stared Harrison in the eye. 'Tell me, Dr Harris, when you saw Candida in the hut, what were you thinking?'

'That's easy, Dr Andrews –' He tucked a stray curl away from her forehead. 'I wished it was you, and that I was Ryan.'

Somehow ignoring the presence of his shaft as it dug at her thigh, and with a suggestive curl of her lips, Beth got onto all fours, her hair falling over her shoulders, her pulse thumping in her throat. 'Like this?'

'Oh, doll!' Harrison resumed his self-allotted task, and tapped a fingertip over each and every freckle on her exposed back. 'I'm not going to tie you like Candida was, and I'm not gonna blindfold you, but I do want you to stay still. Promise?'

'I'll try.' Beth giggled, knowing there wasn't a hope in hell that she'd be able to remain motionless for long.

With her curls draped over her forehead, she didn't see Harrison pick his find brush back up. 'I believe I was in the middle of an examination,' he reminded her.

'Every single freckle requires a proper look.'

'But I've got thousands of them!' Beth shivered again, her hands enjoying the texture of the wet brush as the torturously beautiful bristles dabbed and smoothed her skin, sending waves of electricity coursing through her body.

In only seconds, she realised she was losing the fight to stay motionless. The brush was moving so slowly, and the tantalizing touch along her back was making her mound and her chest overwhelmingly jealous for some attention of their own.

As her lover reached the dip of her backside, something in Beth snapped. Remembering how Candida had got Ryan's attention, she called, 'Harrison! Please!'

'Please what, doll?'

'Fuck me!'

Harrison swept the brush over her buttocks, joining each orange freckle with the next. 'On one condition.'

'Anything!' Beth could feel her arms begin to shake as he inched the brush closer to her clit, circling it between her open legs without actually touching her need.

'You will apply for the job in Colorado.'

'I promise.' Her breath was becoming shallow as she added, her eyes tightly closed, 'But I might not get it!'

'You might not, but hey, doll, the world is huge. We could both get posts somewhere new.'

Beth couldn't keep the joy from her voice. 'Together?'

Harrison came round to her head, flipped up her fringe, and buried his gaze into her wide green eyes. 'Together.' Then lust regained its control, and the necessity to be inside Beth finally got the better of him. Dropping his brush, he rolled on a condom before grabbing her hips and sinking into Beth's velvet softness with a force that collapsed them both to the floor in a fit of laughing bliss.

With his thickness filling her better than it had any of her fantasies, Beth cried out in desire as Harrison's hands massaged her tits as they swung beneath her. Feeling her chest constrict, she moaned with a pleasure that originated in the back of her throat, and escaped into the night sky, rapidly accompanied by an accompanying grunt of "Hell yes, doll" from Harrison.

Pumping back and forth, Beth revelled in the light spank of Harrison's balls against her flesh as his cock twitched within her. Suddenly, his legs became statute still and, with a sharp squeeze of her right breast and a pinch at her clit, Harrison sent Beth into a body-jacking climax as he came deep within her.

Rolling away quickly before Harrison had the chance to catch his breath, Beth, her chest rising and falling fast, wrapped a towel around her shoulders to deflect some of the chilled night air before pointing to the centre of the rug. Picking up the discarded brush, she said, 'Your turn.'

'Doll?'

Putting her hands on her naked hips, Beth winked at him. 'Dr Harris, I was under the impression we were *co-*supervisors, which means what I do you do. It would therefore be terribly unprofessional of me not to explore your body as thoroughly as you've investigated mine.' She flicked the soft bristles between her fingers. 'Don't you agree?'

THE END

More from Kay Jaybee:

Xcite
www.xcitebooks.com

To join our mailing list scan the QR code